Time Doctors #5

Time Kicks Back

Jacky Gray

To the wonderful Bletchley people, past and present.

Find out more at:
https://jroauthor.co.uk/
https://hengistpeoplehorse.blogspot.co.uk/
https://www.facebook.com/HengistPeopleOfTheHorse

Subscribe to Jacky's newsletter to find out the latest news and deals and receive your FREE Bonus Extras:
https://eepurl.com/b5ZScH

Contents

Prologue – Spidey Senses

In many ways, Kev's entire life had been leading up to this moment.

Admittedly, not exactly here in this less-than-salubrious pub, 22 years before he was actually born. But to a similar situation where all the life hacks resulting from his upbringing, education, and experiences coalesced. Even the parts he'd played in school productions – thanks to a sympathetic drama teacher recognising his talent for slipping into a skin other than his own – came in handy. He adopted the confidence and sleaze of a 60s spiv, made easier by Georgie's assurance that he rocked the trench coat, fedora and slicked back hair. He'd had a teeny tiny tremor about the etiquette of wearing a hat indoors, and quite what you were supposed to do with the damned thing when you took it off. But Ben's golden advice saw him in good stead – watch what the people around you do, and blend in. He sipped the pale ale with a grimace.

Prickles at the back of his neck and the odd snatched phrase alerted him to the increasing interest of a nearby table of thugs. He'd clocked them as the power centre in the room while at the bar, the mirror behind it being perfectly placed for that function. He mused that its original purpose was to make the mean selection of spirits appear twice the size. Also, given some of the seedy clientele, to give the landlord eyes in the back of his head.

Part of Kev's training involved augmenting his senses to lessen his chances of being taken by surprise, and they were ganging up to inform him now would be a good time to bug out. He'd learnt as much as he could from this particular watering hole, and was unlikely to gain any further information about his prey by sticking around. Several bruises and the odd cracked rib, maybe, but they'd have to catch him first.

He made his move and, by the time they entered the alley, he was ready for them.

Ch 1 – Paranoid Much?

July 2022

Kev hadn't been oblivious to his housemates' references to *Bodysnatcher*-style pods in the greenhouse in a recent discussion about him and Isaac. He'd just chosen not to bite – more evidence that an alien had indeed taken over his body. Or in his gran's words, he was finally starting to act his age instead of his shoe size.

That was about right. Since their first meeting, Isaac's smug superiority and relentless digs made Kev want to stick his tongue out and waggle his fingers in his ears like an eight-year-old. Except the guy had definitely undergone some kind of brain surgery in the past few weeks which suppressed his alien self. To the point where he'd stopped behaving like a giant pain-in-the-arse at home and even – shock, horror – been complimentary at work. And not just to Kev, some of the other guys had commented.

Oso, the deputy team leader who'd been Isaac's regular target before Kev's arrival, collared him after their joint review meeting. "So who was that and what've you done with the real Isaac?"

With a snort, Kev assured him of the lack of pods.

Tapping the side of his nose, Oso nodded toward Jen's desk where Isaac had stopped on his way past. "Could the gorgeous Jen have anything to do with it? Shame, I thought she had better taste in men."

"Until you tried it on and she gave you the elbow?"

They both turned away from her fierce glare and Oso winked. "Me and every other guy in here. The book still has her 50-1 as AC/DC." A hopeful glance.

"My lips are sealed, mate. Not my place."

"But you *live* with her. Who else is gonna tell all?" He nudged him. "They were spotted getting cosy at Spoons."

"One breakfast. Once. To research some D&D stuff."

"Watching them like a hawk, much?"

"Behave. I have no romantic interest in Jen Paulson."

A wink. "So she marked your card, too. I knew it."

Bugger. His lips quirked as his mind used her favourite swear word – a throwback to the fifties when it was considered the height of depravity. *Simpler times*. Oso's grin said he was enjoying the idea of her rejection far too much. Kev had learnt never to add fuel to the fire of a rumour, so he cut it dead, returning to his desk.

But he lacked the concentration to deal with the actions arising from the meeting and picked up his mug, heading for the kitchen to make a brew.

"Enough for two in there?" The smile in Jen's voice said she wasn't there by accident.

"Of course. Tea or coffee?"

"If you're having tea, I'll share the bag."

"I know – you don't like it too strong. Done." He took the offered mug, inwardly cringing from the dancing eyes which saw straight through his insouciance. But after so many months mooning after her, and at least as many living with her, he'd finally come around to the conclusion he just wasn't her type. *And never could be*. She needed more.

"Kev." A pause long enough to make him meet her gaze. "Is everything all right?"

He frowned. "Sure. Why wouldn't it be?"

4

A shrug. "I remember how it was when we finished *Tangled Warren*. After spending every waking minute living and breathing scenes, maps and devilish clues, it left a massive hiatus in my life. Took me a while to get back into something approaching normality."

"Whatever that is."

She grinned. "True. Ours is not exactly your average, run-of-the-mill household."

"Unless you live in Hawkins, Indiana." He knew she'd get the *Stranger Things* reference.

"Or Sunnydale, California."

"With *Buffy* and the Scoobies." He chuckled. "Or Halliwell Manor."

"Wait, *Charmed*? Didn't know you were a fan."

"You're kidding, right? Three gorgeous gals and a host of monsters? What's not to like?"

A grin. "Anyway, the point is, we don't see much of you these days, you're always huddled up with Isaac."

"When *you're* not, you mean?" Jealousy made that came out far too quickly and he was glad of the excuse to make the tea as the kettle boiled.

She'd got the milk from the fridge, but held it just out of reach until he glanced at her and asked "What?"

"If you have a comment, man up and say it."

With a shrug, he stretched for the milk. "None of my business how you choose to spend your time."

"You got that right. Nor who with."

"It's just …" *How could he put this without offending her?* "Knowing both of you reasonably well, I wouldn't exactly say it's an obvious match."

"Georgie's right. It *is* all about sex with you."

"She said that?" *Ouch. Surely she knew him better after sharing the same house for so long.*

"Admittedly it was a while ago, but some things don't change. Bit more milk in mine, please."

"Sorry, did I make it too strong? I know you prefer dishwater strength." He passed her the mug.

"My fault for giving you a hard time." A grin. "So what's gone on to make you and Isaac BFFs? Bit of a change from the normal knives out."

"I'll give you three guesses."

"That's easy. D&D, gaming and old war movies. Or possibly Star Trek."

"Right on all counts. He nurses a notion he can beat me in a shoot-em-up game." A snort. "Never gonna happen."

"Fair enough. And it was obvious he gave you a bunch of help with your *Cursed Castle* campaign."

"Not as much as you might think. In actual–"

"Are you two gonna do any work today?" Oso strode up, tapping his watch pointedly.

"*Do what?*" Kev grinned, slapping him on the back. "Pots and kettles, mate. Your reputation as the biggest consumer of coffee remains unchallenged."

He leaned forward. "Heads up. There be customers in the vicinity, and you know how management like to give the impression we're chained to our workstations 24-7."

"Prat." The opposite was normally true, but Kev could do with a few brownie points, so he hustled to his desk, ploughing straight into the updates. But a wee niggle at the back of his mind couldn't help wondering about Jen's motives. It was – unusual, at the very least – for her to say more than a sentence to him unless it was something job-related; she maintained a purely professional façade with all the guys at work. On any other girl, the combination of concern, warm smiles and subtle teasing could have been construed as flirting, but this was Jen, for goodness' sake.

Taking a swig of tea, he caught sight of the director with a couple of suits and bent his head to the task in hand. *Not the right time to be staring into the middle distance.*

Things took a positively surreal turn later when he spotted Isaac's planner on his desk. *WTF?* The guy never went anywhere without it – surely he would have spotted it missing by now – wouldn't he? Checking his watch, Kev reasoned it was nearly lunch and Isaac's office was on the way to the canteen. Sounded like a good excuse for beating the queue – their curry day was always popular.

Surreal because he never expected a thank you, let alone an apology for putting him out. *Was he on something?*

"Let me buy you lunch – it's curry today."

"There's no need." *Really. None at all.*

"Obviously not, but I want to pick your brains."

Okay, this had gone way beyond weird. Kev was thinking lobotomy in the very least.

But it was nothing to do with work. Kev's recent Dungeons and Dragons scenario had been anything but conventional. Isaac wanted to understand how he'd handled certain aspects, particularly the general playing rules. It became clear he was planning something on similar lines.

"There's a scenario I've always wanted to run but hadn't a clue how to massage it into the normal format."

"Give me a clue. Is it something to do with Star Trek?"

"I couldn't possibly say."

"Star Wars then. Or Firefly? Some kind of sci-fi?"

"Absolutely not. The exact opposite."

"Aha. Historical." Kev kept going. Given his major passions, it didn't take a genius to figure it out. "A film-noir gumshoe? World War One? Or Two?"

He raised his hands. "I'm not going to tell you. But please, don't breathe a word to the others."

Back at his desk, Kev tried to focus on work, but his mind preferred to dwell on what had begun to take on almost sinister overtones. As he'd hinted to Jen, Isaac *had* given him a few pointers to set up his *Cursed Castle* campaign – God knew, he needed all manner of assistance to deal with such a massive undertaking. Although he'd noticed how Isaac's suggestions resulted in opportunities for his player to come off as a hero. Usually at the detriment of Ben's. But the fact she'd brought it up rang alarm bells as a number of covert glances between the others flashed past his mind's eye.

The ones between Ben and Georgie whenever he found them alone together could be explained by the romantic liaison he was convinced they were enjoying, despite their protests. But lately, Jen seemed to have joined their huddle. His brain replayed a recent episode in the kitchen of the mansion they all shared. She'd blown a fuse, talking like someone off an old black-and-white movie and shot off. The others had put it down to work pressure and lack of sleep, but there had definitely been an undercurrent. He shook his head. What was that saying? *Just because you're paranoid doesn't mean they're not out to get you.* Or something similar.

After dinner, Isaac suggested they resume their previous bout, but when they got to the gaming room, he questioned how Kev had handled the real-life historical stuff.

"Do you not remember the background info in the starter pack?"

"I mean after that."

Kev tried to explain, but Isaac, being Isaac, wanted specific details.

"All the notes are on my laptop."

"Well go fetch it." The old Isaac's entitled tone had Kev's hackles prickling.

He caught himself on with a rueful gesture. "Sorry. *Please* could you get it? If it's not too much trouble."

He'd gone completely the other way and his humility grated almost as much, but Kev got up anyway.

As he approached the lounge, he heard the other three talking in the kind of low voices which suggested a huddle. The door was ajar and he figured he needed to be stealthier than normal – they always seemed to hear him coming.

The paranoid thought returned, so he crept closer, feeling like a spy in one of Isaac's beloved forties films. Straining to hear Jen's dulcet tones, he wondered idly whether the glass against the wall thing actually worked.

Ben's question about what she'd discovered could have meant anything.

She scoffed. "I think he was about to say something relevant but Oso interrupted."

They were definitely talking about him. He had to stop the sharp intake of breath which could have given it away, but his outrage meant he only heard part of Ben's next question. "… you get anywhere?"

Georgie's voice sounded strained. "I told you I'm no Mata Hari. I'll be a lot happier when we let Kev into the secret. It doesn't seem fair–"

Kev had heard enough, bursting in to face three guilty expressions. "What secret? I *knew* you lot were up to something." He glared at Jen. "And what was all that nonsense at work? You were obviously on some kind of undercover mission, flirting like a cheap–"

"Kev. Catch yourself on. There's no way of finishing that sentence which doesn't hurt." Ben glared.

Rubbing his hands over his face, Kev reined it in, peering at Jen. "Sorry, Pet. I guess I've been feeling a bit marginalised by you guys."

Jen smiled. "Sorry. We didn't mean to. Like I said, he seems to be your new bestie and we didn't want to put you in the awkward position of having to be disloyal to him."

"Now I'm getting worried. What could you possibly have found out about him?" Again with the undercurrent as Ben and Georgie tried to hide their alarm.

Jen was cucumber cool. "He's probably already told you, but I figured out what he's been doing on Fridays."

He frowned. "No he hasn't. Go on then, tell all."

She glanced at the other two, who nodded. Kev couldn't decide how much of their expressions were pure relief.

"He's been taking driving lessons. I saw him getting into a driving school car."

10

"Seriously? That's it? All this intrigue because he's finally learning to drive?"

"What intrigue?" Ben's attempt at innocence didn't quite cut it. "It's your overactive imagination, mate."

"Probably too much time rocking up all those intense storylines about spies and stuff in the *Cursed Castle*."

Kev tried to treat Georgie's comment with the same lightness she'd delivered it, but struggled to shake the feeling they were closing ranks; playing him for a sucker. *A game he knew well*. Rolling his eyes, he left them with a "whatever" and went upstairs to retrieve his laptop.

On his return, the TV was blasting out the theme tune to something he vaguely recognised, and he walked past, trying to believe they really weren't conspiring against him.

The last thing he needed was Isaac's overdeveloped distrust, but that's what he got for his sins. It did put his own misgivings into perspective and, when he went over the whole day in his head, he reflected that no way did he want to end up with that level of obsessive suspicion.

The following evening saw Isaac unleashing his idea, starting with an almost apology.

"I hope you'll bear with me as I've not got the hang of how this one will play out. It's going to be hard enough without you inventing all sorts of characters so I've taken the liberty of designing some for you. But you can at least choose which one you like most from these four."

"Just a sec. Are you saying I don't get to rock up my character?"

Georgie grinned. "Stop whinging, Kev. You were only

11

saying last time how you wanted something other than the comic relief. Think of this as an opportunity. How about playing the hero for a change?

He skip-read the brief of the character she handed to him, realising he was yet again being suckered in. But actually … "Okay, I'll give it a go."

"Well unless we're gender bending I guess I'm playing a professor. Again." Ben grumbled as he rifled through the remaining characters.

Jen made a grab for one of the remaining two. "The debutante for me please. The other one sounds like a right old dogsbody." She flashed an apologetic look at Georgie.

"Hettie's not a dogsbody. Her job's one of the most important."

"Inter-office messenger sounds like a dogsbody to me."

"Au contraire – she's the only one with the whole picture. Read on."

Georgie quickly picked it up before Jen could change her mind. "That's more like it. Oohhh–"

"Exactly." A knowing wink.

Jen glanced up. "What is it?"

"You can't know." With an infuriating smirk, Isaac handed a second sheet of paper to everyone. "These are things only your character knows. And as I'm already bending the rules out of shape to run this, I've decided to give you all a secret goal." He watched in satisfaction as several eyes widened as they scanned through their sheet. "I've always wanted to do that actually. This seems like the perfect scenario to do it."

Jen glanced up. "This is quite a cool idea. Do we get to

know each other's objectives?"

"No. Keyword is *secret*. The whole point is nobody's supposed to know anything about what the others are doing. If you'd read the important notice in the red box–"

"Oh, that. I thought it only applied when we started."

Isaac shook his head, his tone heavy with exasperation. "This is why I've never attempted this scenario before. I knew you wouldn't take it seriously."

"Don't sulk." Only Ben could get away with saying that. "If you'd said the warning applied to session zero, we'd have got it. But I don't see how it's going to work–"

"That's the big problem. We've never done anything where the players didn't all work as a team. It might be a huge disaster from the start."

Ben clapped him on the back. "Nonsense. If we could make Kev's unconventional effort work, I'm sure this will be a piece of cake."

Georgie shot him a glare and he winked back.

"Famous last words." Kev refused to admit how much the exchange affected him, let alone try to understand why.

Isaac cleared his throat. "Let's start. You've all been invited for interviews for various roles at the Bletchley Park estate. The year is 1940 and Hitler's war machine is rolling across Europe. Kev, you're up first. Everyone else, go grab a brew."

Ch 2 – Setting the Scene

GC&CS - Spring 1940

 Clive Thompson (Kev) – an ex-RAF war-hero

 Edward Foster (Ben) – a Cambridge mathematician

 The Spymaster (Isaac) – the dungeon master

 June Cavendish (Jen) – a sparky debutante

 Hettie Bartley (Georgie) – a young clerk

Clive tapped his teeth with a nail, a rhythm he'd been told sounded like Morse code for "sm." He'd acquired the nervous habit while sitting in the cockpit of a Spitfire, waiting for the off. This time it wasn't the "chocks away" he awaited, but the pleasure of an extremely important man referred to only as "C."

The doorknob turned and before the door had swung open more than a couple of inches, Clive was on his feet, arm raised in an automatic salute as the previous guy came out, leaving the door open. Keeping his gaze directed at the floor, the man shambled past in a jumble of barnyard hair, patched tweed and pipe tobacco.

Holding the pose took effort as the thin-faced man at the desk finished writing and closed the buff folder, placing it on a large pile as he raised his head.

His gaze pierced and his tone anticipated compliance. "At ease, Flight Lieutenant. Come in, take a seat."

Barely using his walking stick, Clive moved as quickly as his injury allowed, attempting to minimise the limp.

"Don't bother trying to disguise it. For the job I have in mind, the hobbling will be a perfect cover. The women will want to mother you and the men will write you off as no physical threat. It will give us a distinct advantage."

Sitting and standing were both challenging, but not having to mask the pain made it considerably easier. Clive took his time, hoping this sharp, formidable man would enlighten him sooner rather than later.

Fat chance. The detailed delve into his training, missions and the incident which had led to enforced resignation from active service kept Clive on his toes as he gave short, honest answers to each question.

With the grilling over, the man sat back, his expression impassive. "Before joining the air force, you studied engineering at Manchester University, I believe."

"Correct."

"And you tinker with automobiles and motorcycles?"

"Yes." He curbed his instinct to enthuse.

"Do you consider yourself a joiner, Thompson?"

"Sir?" He raised a brow.

No humour invaded the short bark. "Nothing to do with woodwork. I mean the sort of man who feels the need to spend his leisure time in the pursuit of social activities."

"That would depend."

"Wrong answer. If you were to succeed, you'd have to lose your reticence and become the life and soul of every party from football to fencing and cricket to Scottish reels." He gestured at the walking cane with a grimace. "At least, that was the plan. But you should be able to manage with bridge, chess and the choral society."

"I suspect they'd soon mark me out as a growler."

Frowning, the man flicked his eyes to the large pile.

Clive figured he'd blown it, shrugging. "If there's a

book club I read a lot."

"Not currently. I can't see you in the drama club."

"Actually, I did a few productions at school."

He sat forward. "Promising. They're auditioning for a new show right now. A Shakespeare, I believe."

"The last one I did was Much Ado. I like the comedies."

"Well that's just tipped you over the edge. Our three main suspects are all thespians. But I don't want to do your job for you." He went on to give a brief outline of what the job would entail.

When he exited the room, Clive's head whirled with the enormity of the role he was about to play. National security was but a small part. *No pressure, then*.

In his role as Spymaster, Isaac decreed each of them should go through the interview process in isolation so they wouldn't be privy to the other's backstory. Kev couldn't see it working, but they'd all taken *his* weird ideas on board, so he owed it to them to try. He flopped down on the sofa in the lounge. "Your turn Georgie."

Jen glanced up from her phone. "Have you tried the Enigma app? It's quite cool."

"Not yet. Can't get it to load."

"That's because you have so much junk on your phone. You need to have a clear out. Here, watch this."

As they crowded around Jen's iPhone, Georgie reappeared. "Ben next."

"Blimey, you were quick."

"Because the interview process for an office dogsbody is short." A wink. "Reckon I chose the right one."

Shortly afterwards, the session began in earnest.

~>#<~

The four recruits scanned the rather grand room which had obviously been hastily converted into an office. Nerves had them surreptitiously peeking at the other three successful candidates, wondering how they'd fared in the stringent interview. A fierce-looking chap strode in and introduced himself as Commander Denniston.

"Welcome to Bletchley Park. You've all signed the Official Secrets Act, and there's a good reason why that was the first thing you did when you arrived here. You will all have an important part to play to help us win this war. You'll maintain confidentiality in everything you do, and you will *not* pry into what anybody else does. Or you'll find yourself sitting out the rest of the war in a military prison. Do I make myself absolutely clear?" Nods.

"You'll need to be especially careful of the householders where you are billeted. We've already had to move a couple of people because their landlord asked too many questions. If you can't put them off with bland answers, let us know. Same goes for your own family. Miss Molesworth in the admin office has a list of replies which deter most people from probing too deeply."

He addressed Hettie directly. "As you may have gathered, every person who works here is valuable, and your job is one of the most important. This site couldn't function without communication and the quicker the better. As I've said, we have strict rules that no person should know anything apart from what goes on in their particular section. However, messages need to be passed rapidly

17

between huts and that will be your responsibility."

"No wonder you were asking about how fast I can run – I thought it was a bit odd."

He glanced at his watch "That's it for you, Miss Bartley. If you'd like to report to Miss Molesworth, she will introduce you to the other messengers and take you through your duties."

Clive watched her leave the room, trying to decipher the expression on her face. Denniston became grim. "Everything in Bletchley Park is on a need-to-know basis and she doesn't need to know the next bit."

The other two swapped a glance, and Clive made a mental note of their reactions as the commander continued.

"Hitler's success in invading Poland owed a lot to technological advances. Each infantry unit had an attached Panzer division which burst through the enemy's defences, supported by pilots in dive-bombing Stukas."

"That's tanks and planes." The blonde woman's chin jutted as she sought confirmation.

"Correct, Miss Cavendish. The essence of the so-called Blitzkrieg technique is 'speed of attack through speed of communications.' Which in the field means radio signals."

"So anyone can pick it up." June shrugged. "Assuming they know Morse code."

"Quite. Specially trained signallers accompany the ground and air forces on their fast-moving rampage, and we believe they're targeting the whole of Europe just as they did twenty-five years ago."

The tall chap in a leather-patched tweed jacket snorted. "So much for the Munich agreement, let alone Versailles."

"No point crying over spilt milk, Foster. Our monumental task requires total focus and commitment from each of you." He displayed a photograph. "They're doing it by using command vehicles like this one, and in the bottom left you can see a machine which looks like a typewriter, but every key press is encoded to a different letter."

"Like a Caesar code?" June shrugged. "Surely that's breakable by studying letter frequencies."

He produced a close up photo of the machine, pointing to three wheels. "Each one adds a level of encoding, which means multiplying by twenty six, and there are other complications giving over a hundred and fifty million trillion possibilities for each letter. Aka a quintillion."

"How many zeros is that?"

"Eighteen after the one fifty – although it's actually closer to 159. Oh, and the settings which determine the encryption are changed every day at midnight."

She sat back, deflated.

"However, we have a head start. Our codebreakers, led by an extremely clever man, Dilly Knox, have determined strategies which bring us closer to solving this puzzle. That's why you're here – you will *all* have a vital part to play in the success of this venture. As I said, secrecy is imperative–"

"I'm assuming that's why all my post has to go to a London box number." Edward sucked on an empty pipe.

"And why I have to tell anyone who asks I'm just a boring typist." Despite her neutral tone, June drew a glare from Denniston.

"If anyone asks you about GC and CS, you say it's the

19

Golf, Cheese and Chess Society – it should put them off."

"What if it doesn't?" Edward asked an instant before June asked what it really stood for. He ignored them both.

After a brief outline of the process, he revealed how, contrary to popular belief that Hitler's Enigma machines were impregnable, Polish codebreakers had made great headway in 1938. "But on December 15th, the Germans added another two wheels, so instead of just six combinations of the three wheels, there are now sixty."

June sat back and Clive could tell she was itching to check this as she scribbled a note on her pad. "Did they know the Poles had broken the code, is that why they added the extra wheels?"

"It's possible. But I only told you to make you extra cautious. You've been assigned to the decoding room."

"So I'll be working on the decryptions?" She almost clapped her hands.

"No, that's done in the machine room. You'll be with the other girls typing the messages on a modified Typex machine–"

"Wait. Have I got this straight? The machine room is where the decoding is done, and the decoding room is full of machines."

His glare dialled up a couple of notches, even as his tone sank way below freezing. "If you continue to make such fatuous remarks I can have you cleaning toilets. You've tried my patience to its limits." He pointed to the door. "Go. Find Miss Molesworth and ask her to put you down for the Typex course."

She hadn't even reached the door as he grumbled, "Why

they insist on sending silly debs …" With a tut, he sat forward. "You two will both be involved in the decryption – there is a short course, but I'll give you a brief overview to get you started."

Some of it went over Clive's head, but he figured he'd catch up as soon as he started handling the thing – he was more practical than cerebral. Edward didn't say much, just sat there sucking on the empty pipe; the moist sound grating on Clive's taut nerves.

At the end, Denniston shook their hands, wishing them well, but as Clive followed Edward, he called him back, gesturing for him to close the door. "After the course, you'll start with a team whose remit is to gather information about each part of the process in order to assess for expansion. It's ideal because it will give you a good overview and a reason for going into every hut and observing."

"But I thought no one person should possess all the data in case they were captured."

"A good idea in principle, but it can lead to the embarrassing situation we had last year when one of our boffins ended up reinventing a vital wheel."

"Surely that wouldn't be a problem if it's vital."

"Except his time would have been far better spent on his current project – we'd be a lot further on by now."

"Is this the man I'll be working for by any chance?"

A nod. "But I must impress on you the importance of not revealing your true purpose."

Following the directions, Clive hobbled over to Hut 6, joining Gordon Welchman's small team. The man could have been Edward's brother, with matching moustache and pipe, but he replaced the guarded reticence with friendly enthusiasm. The exact opposite of spy material.

Instantly this flagged a warning in Clive's mind. The short course "C" had him attend to sharpen his observational and deductive skills, had opened his mind about typical spy behaviour. His natural instincts pointed to Edward's wary reserve – the guy studied everything and everyone as though there might be a test later. But the instructor suggested a true spy wouldn't be so obvious; charming smiles and an open demeanour would conceal his covert information-gathering. "A consummate actor who'd likely join several societies to select and groom his targets." *A joiner*.

Clive clawed back his focus as his new boss introduced his assistants Pat and Peg, who logged the time and frequency information on a daily chart from the preamble of each enigma message as it arrived by teleprinter. Once he'd identified the discriminants, they colour coded them to show the traffic type.

"You mean like the red traffic for the Luftwaffe?" His brain had very little capacity for new stuff, but he was glad something had stuck from the session with Denniston.

"Except it's actually for co-ordinating between army and air-force, but the fly-boys are a tad trigger happy. Yellow is principally for the invasion of Norway, and we're trying to understand the brown and orange, too."

"What happens when you run out of colours?"

"Don't mock." Gordon glowered. "We actually ran out of coloured pencils at one point, but I found a stack in our previous home, left behind from when it was Elmers school."

"That was lucky." *But it doesn't answer my question.*

"As to your original question." A beat. "We'll probably go for flowers or birds. The Naval guys in Hut 8 use sea animals like dolphin." He started describing the technique for using rods to search for cribs, however Clive had reached saturation point and nothing was sticking.

"I can see your eyes are glazing over – it's rather a lot to take in on the first day." He glanced at his watch. "Where are you billeted?"

He named the pub in a village south of Bletchley.

"Excellent. A short walk to the Duncombe Arms where I'm staying. The landlord's an absolute brick – lets us use his billiards room as an unofficial social club."

~*~

Isaac suggested they join the others for a short comfort break. They were in the lounge with an opened bottle of wine and two glasses on the table. As Georgie jumped up to pour theirs, Isaac regarded her thoughtfully. "I'm sorry your character got dismissed from the briefing so early. I'm still trying to figure out how to best do all the need-to-know stuff. I hope you weren't too bored waiting."

"That's fine. I told you, there's some crap going on at work and I suspect the brown stuff's gonna hit the whirling blades any moment which means I won't be available. So not having to be a part of every scene might be a blessing."

"Everything okay, Pet?" Kev had never known anything but harmony concerning her idyllic job looking after the town's green spaces.

"Just a problem with those dratted floral displays."

"The ones you did for the jubilee? I drove past one the other day and it's definitely past its best."

"Because of that heatwave. A stack of the irrigation units failed and we couldn't water them fast enough."

"That's a shame, but it's all over now so you can start again with fresh designs."

"That's the trouble. The council thought they were being smart with re-use because of the Commonwealth Games at the end of the month. But now we're in a pickle because of supply problems due to the extreme temperatures, so I may have to end up raiding garden centres to get the right coloured flowers."

"Sounds like a lot of hassle." Kev sipped the wine, enjoying the rich, velvety texture.

"You don't know the half of it. A couple of the planting team have gone down with this latest bug and from what I can gather it's virtually a certainty I'll cop for it."

Isaac sniffed, shuffling to the other side of the sofa.

"Don't worry. I'm still testing negative."

"I don't have a lot of faith in them–"

"Oh for God's sake, grow a pair." Kev glowered. "It wouldn't be the worst thing in the world if you finally caught a dose. It's so bloody tame now, you've probably had it and not even known."

"But I would know–"

"How? That cold you haven't got rid of since May–"

"I haven't had a cold."

"So why are you always sniffing?" Kev turned to the others. "Tell me you've noticed it too? Drives me dotty."

"Like anyone would know the difference." Ben got in a split-second before Georgie's, "Dotty? What *have* you been watching?"

Jen huffed a heavy sigh. "Kev's missing the point completely. It's reached the point now that you're actually better off if you do get it because it reduces the chances of getting it again."

"Sez who?" Isaac sniffed, cutting it off abruptly.

Kev gestured an "I rest my case your honour" shrug, while Jen's glare bristled with, "Tell him" energy. But now was not the time. "Whoever I quote, you'll just throw a bunch of dodgy, so-called facts the government are still desperate to use to cover all the rubbish mandates. I'd rather hear what the others think of your show so far."

Ben chuckled. "Much as I fall easily into the role, I'm in danger of getting typecast. Two Oxbridge professors in a row? *Am I really that boring?* Don't answer that."

"You have hogged the hero/leader role for a while."

"Which you can't have any complaints about." Georgie grinned at Kev. "It's definitely the Kev and Isaac show. Just like the last one. But if we have to sit out each time, we might start a rival group."

Isaac's hands blurred as though trying to erase the idea. "I'm sure it won't happen all the time. There's bound to be opportunities for you all to interact – especially in the social scenes. It doesn't have to be secrets and skulduggery all the time. I reckon we could pass notes for some of the private stuff so nobody has to leave the room. I'm sure you'll all have plenty to do."

"I'll believe that when I see it." Jen's tone mocked.

"I'm not sure about my character. I've read a few books in the area and the whole thing about silly debutantes–"

"Well, it's up to you what your character does. Apart from the sexist attitudes, what did you think?"

"Jury's out. But if I get to do some actual decoding, I reckon I'll enjoy it."

"Let's see how it pans out. I know you all love a good spy spoof, so there's scope for snooping, cracking secret codes and wheedling out traitors. Where first?"

"This social club Gordon mentioned will let us get a feel for the place. How about there?" Ben scanned around, getting nods, so Kev said he'd meet them in five.

When he arrived at the pub later that evening, Clive walked through the fog of cigarette smoke to the bar, where he was served with a pint of watered-down beer and directed to "follow the racket." The large back room sported three billiards tables and a couple of dart boards, both well attended by enthusiastic spectators cheering on their favourites. Welchman stood with a cue at one of the tables, groaning as his opponent pulled off a tricky shot, lining the cue up behind his back. This stroke won the game, and after a sporting handshake, Welchman introduced his opponent to Clive as Dennis Babbage, a friend from Cambridge. "You should meet Frank Birch – he's the one who made this place what it is."

Frank held court in a corner, surrounded by several eager young things hanging on his every word as he regaled with tales of his Widow Twankey in pantomime.

A striking red-head passed him a clipboard bearing a

sheet which he signed with a grumble. She batted her eyes. "I heard you were in a BBC play on TV last year."

"Quite so. I hope all of you will be auditioning for my next production."

"Will it be like the Alice in Wonderland satire you wrote at the end of the Great War?" One of the girls with her back to Clive asked.

"Alice in ID25? You're well informed, young lady. No, this is my adaptation of *Much Ado About Nothing*. I promise it will be full of romance and comedy."

"Will you be playing the lead?" The red-head again.

"Hardly. I shall direct and, if we can't get sufficient good men, I may take a small part." He glanced up, spotting Clive. "And who have we here?"

"Thompson. Clive Thompson."

Next to Birch, a dapper man in a bow-tie glanced up. "I like that, it has a sharp ring. Good voice, too."

A snort. "Fleming has a good ear. Part of being a journalist." Birch gestured at Clive. "What say you, ladies? A leading man if ever I saw one. Tell me you can act."

He shrugged. "I dabbled a bit at college."

"Excellent. Sit there."

The dark-haired girl squashed up to make room and he recognised Hettie.

She giggled as he squeezed in next to her, raising a glass. "Welcome to the Drunken Arms."

He clinked glasses with a grin. "Very apt."

"Hello again." Edward called from the other side of Hettie. He'd lost the pipe and the rosy flush said he'd been there a while. "We new bods should stick together." He sat back and Clive spotted June behind him.

She drew on the cigarette in an elegant holder and blew out the smoke, her eyes hooded.

"June, isn't it? The anything-but-silly deb. I wish I'd given the pompous sod an earful."

"Don't get in a tizz. I'm perfectly capable of standing up for myself when I choose to. It's a matter of picking the right battles. No point ruffling feathers till I've uncovered the true source of power here."

"That makes perfect sense." *And was quite revealing.* Clive had learnt not to stare, but rather take a snapshot in his mind and turn away to study it for the subtle tells.

"I'll drink to that." Edward sipped his beer. "In fact, tonight, I'll drink to anything. I'm glad to have made it through the first day, even if my brains are scrambled."

"Like an Enigma code? I'll have it sussed in a day."

Clive had no doubt the feisty girl would, but the prickling on the side of his face, alerted him to someone's scrutiny. Suppressing the instinct to turn, he gauged the direction while apparently giving all his attention to his three new friends. Depositing his half-empty glass on the table, his peripheral vision clocked the observer.

The shrewd gaze as Birch assessed this influx of new people reminded Clive of a phrase used by the instructor on the spy course. "His biggest talent would be charming everyone to believe he was harmless, trustworthy friend material instead of a ruthless, cold-blooded manipulator." *It fit Birch to a "T."*

Ch 3 – Secrets and Codes

July 2022/April 1940

Sunday's session started with some brainstorming of what they'd learned so far.

"This play sounds important. And Ian Fleming being involved got my spy-der senses tingling." Ben chuckled.

As the others groaned, Jen shot back. "As Much Ado as that was a terrible pun, I think he's probably right."

"We should ignore it – that'll really mess up the DMs plans!" Kev's quip earnt a murderous look from Isaac.

Georgie sighed. "We should sign up for the auditions Birch mentioned. But what do we do in the meantime?"

"As I said yesterday, I want to learn more about decoding. This *is* Bletchley Park, after all. Can we do something to see where our characters fit in?"

"I'm glad you asked." Isaac perked up. "I prepared something just in case. I've got some short scenes to run you through your duties." He'd organised it cleverly to follow several of the steps in the message path Denniston had described.

The first scene had Hettie collecting the bundles from the dispatch riders and delivering them to Hut 8 for naval traffic and Hut 6 for army and air force. She'd no sooner finished than her mobile buzzed with the message she'd been expecting and she disappeared.

On Clive's turn, Welchman told him how they'd built up a picture of the vast radio networks from considering the preamble data at the start of each intercept. He showed the map with lots of little flags. "It allowed us to deduce information about troop position without even decoding the body of the message."

"Clever stuff."

"Indeed. We determined blue traffic is used exclusively as training exercises for the operators and green is for army administration. We believe Hitler has a separate system again, but of course, I don't know a lot about it."

Edward's turn was spent in the sheet-stacking room, poring over large sheets with holes punched through which reduced the number of possible rotor combinations to a manageable number. When he got two potential clicks, he tried it on the Enigma machine app to see if the day's code was broken. On the first one, the output didn't give any recognisable German words anywhere in the first few lines, so it was back to the drawing board.

Jeffreys, the man responsible for designing the sheets, suggested a small adjustment, and lo and behold, it worked.

"Beginner's luck, well done. Note the settings and pass the message to the delightful debs in the decoding room."

Which happened to be where June landed on her turn. Under the watchful eye of the supervisor, she set up her machine, choosing the appropriate rotors and turning each to the correct ring setting before inserting it in the designated position. She connected each of the ten pairs on the "stecker board," according to the chart.

"So now it's ready to use?"

"Not quite. First you find the indicator by typing the first six letters of the main message."

She typed in WQSEUP. "It reads RCMRCM."

"Good. Adjust the rotors till RCM appears in windows. Now you're ready to go."

As she typed in the message, it appeared in the box under the keyboard, the narrator gave a brief insight.

In the field, the Enigma machines merely lit up letters which another operator copied down and then transmitted. Our more sophisticated Typex machines output a long strip of paper containing the decoded German words in a continuous stream. Once the operator – almost exclusively female – had typed in the entire thing, she had to split up the decoded tickertape and glue it on the back of the original message. She'd then pass it through a tunnel to Hut 3 for translation and redrafting to disguise the fact the info had come from an enigma transmission.

As he spoke, Georgie slid into her seat to take her turn.

One of Hettie's regular tasks was to take bundles of messages from Hut 3 to the teleprinter room to be sent to command HQ. She was on strict instructions not to look at them and, as she left there was a pile of scrap for Hut 6. Paper was a precious commodity, and every inch of unused paper was carefully torn off so the boffins could use both sides for their meticulous calculations.

Rounding the corner, someone bumped into her, scattering the pile over the ground. He swooped down in an ill-disguised attempt to "help" her.

On Clive's next turn, he left the hut to see Hettie pleading with a tall man who held her at arm's length while he examined a piece of paper.

"I'm telling you it's blank, they all are. It's nothing but

scrap for Hut 6."

"Well make sure you pick up every piece, you clumsy girl." He stalked off, swaggering with his own importance.

Clive hurried over, disturbed to see the tears in her eyes. "Who was that bully? Did he hurt you?"

"N – no, he just frightens me a bit."

"Really? Who is he?"

"Mr Harrington. He's a boss in the accounts section. None of the girls like him, he's always shouting at them."

"You seem a little shaken. Can I buy you a cuppa?"

"I have to deliver this – they're always running out."

"I'll wait, I'm in no hurry." He watched her dash into Hut 6, reappearing moments later, and repeated his offer.

"I shouldn't really – my break's not for ten minutes."

"Miss M won't mind if I tell her what happened."

"Oh, no. You mustn't do that; she'll have a go at me."

"You can always go back ten minutes early. Come on, I won't take no for an answer."

Shaking her head, she accompanied him, but while they stood in the queue in Hut 2's refreshment counter, she avoided talking by studying the collection of "Careless Talk Costs Lives" posters. One featured a couple in a restaurant leaning forward while Hitler hid under the table writing down what they said. The caption read: "Of course there's no harm in *your* knowing!"

He chuckled. "Pretty funny. But you'd expect nothing less from the art editor of *Punch* magazine."

She wrinkled her nose. "My brother used to get that, but I could never get into it. The cartoons are funny, but the articles are too highfaluting."

"I know what you mean. The political satire is British upper-class stuff – proper poker up its ... you know what."

Giggling, she peered at the next one. "But it's signed Fougasse. That's not British."

"It's Cyril Bird's pen name. He reckoned the Ministry of Information ones were so boring people took no notice."

She nodded. "They're clever the way they make you think of all the different places people could be listening."

They'd reached the front and he pointed to the cakes. "Which do you prefer, a scone or rock cake?"

"I'm not sure there's much of a difference with no butter or jam."

"Two rock cakes it is. At least they're not rock-hard."

As he paid, her attention was drawn by a new poster whose dramatic red background made it stand out. A caricature of Hitler with an outsize ear had the caption "Mr Hitler wants to know!" Underneath this was a poem:

He wants to know the unit's name
Where it's going – whence it came
Ships, guns and shells all make him curious
But silence makes him simply furious.

He nodded at it. "They're hammering the message home. I'm not sure whether to feel irritated or patronised."

"I've never been good at keeping secrets. I hate all these reminders – it makes me feel constantly queasy."

"Because you'd prefer to tell the truth?" He carried the tray to an empty table.

"Exactly. But it's so hard when someone who should know better keeps pressing for me to tell him stuff."

"Would that someone be Harrington by any chance?"

"What makes you say that?"

"Instinct. I don't like bullies."

She shrugged. "He's not actually said much, but it's not the first time I've bumped into him."

"Or he's bumped into you, more likely."

"Do you think so?" She frowned. "Why would he …? Oh!" She whispered, her eyes darting around. "A spy?"

A head shake. "That's not what I meant at all. It's these posters giving you that idea. No, I think his motivation is darker – he simply likes bossing young girls around."

"You're not wrong there. I'm not the only victim of his 'accidental' collisions."

"How do you know this? I suppose you girls warn each other about bullies like him all the time."

"We certainly don't. Miss M would have our guts for garters if we did."

"Except how would she know? I reckon pric–prats like him would get found out sooner if you all swapped tales of his misbehaviour. So how did you find out?"

"When L – one of the girls – mentioned it."

"One of which girls?"

"I can't get her in trouble."

"Fair enough. I respect your loyalty. I suggest you stay out of his way until I can figure out a solution."

She shook her head. "I'm not sure you can help."

A wink. "You'd be surprised. So if he's not the one asking questions, who is?"

"It's the vicar at the house where I'm billeted. But it's not just me; he does it to all of us."

"And you've tried using Miss Molesworth's list of

replies to fend him off."

She glared at him. "Of course. But he just won't give up – it's like some sort of game to him."

"Try a different approach. Start with vague answers, and if he persists, refer back to the messages on the posters. It's easier with an example. Ask where I'm from."

She narrowed her eyes. "Where are you from?"

He gestured. "Up north, where they all speak funny."

"I can tell that from your accent. Northwest, I'd say."

"Yep. A small coastal town you won't have heard of."

"I might. I have relatives up near Blackpool."

"Not that far. How about you? Are you a Brummie?"

"Lots of people say that, but they're much broader than we are." Instead of adding more, she sipped her tea.

"Excellent tactic, but you won't always have tea as an excuse. Is it near Birmingham?"

"Not as close as Solihull. I bet your family love living close to a beach for long walks."

"It's actually quite a walk to the nearest beach. You seem like more of a small town than big city girl."

"Is there a reason for this interrogation?"

"Hello, you two. Mind if we join you?" Edward put down his tray without waiting for an answer.

Clive scanned around to see the place had filled as many of the office girls took their break. "Sure."

As she took her seat, June glanced between them. "I heard some of your chat – is it some sort of game?"

Clive met her gaze. "Not exactly. Hettie's landlord was pushing her about what she did and I was showing her some tricks to get him off her back."

Edward picked up his sausage roll. "If it's so bad, why don't you simply ask for a transfer?" He took a bite.

"Because I've heard tales about the housing officer."

"That he makes girls sit on his knee to get better digs? I heard that, too." June's mouth twisted in disgust.

"And worse." Hettie shuddered.

Clive swapped a dark look with Edward, who put down his food, exclaiming, "I say, that's frightful."

"It seems to be the done thing with some of these petty tyrants they've put in charge." He caught Hettie's pursed lips. "Is there no one else you can ask?"

As she shrugged, June patted her hand. "One of our girls is moving out at the end of the week. Obviously, she couldn't say where she was going, but she thinks it will be for quite a while. If that's any use to you."

"That would be wonderful." Her eyes shone for an instant before dulling. "But it's bound to be against the rules. They're very strict about–"

"This is a matter of national security and they *must* give it priority." Clive tightened his lips, his voice grim. "I'll have a word with the Powers That Be."

"Would you?" Hettie perked up. "I'm sure they'd take a man more seriously."

"They'll listen to me, all right." He took out a notepad, lightening his tone. "I'll need a few details first."

The girls' anxious responses suggested he'd maybe come on a bit strong, so when he'd noted the facts, he got them talking about the possibility of auditioning for Birch's next production.

~*~

Over dinner, they gave Isaac feedback.

Jen started. "It's interesting so far. I'm enjoying learning about the time and place. But I'm not sure what we're supposed to be doing yet."

"Yeah, there's been a lot of scene setting. I'm guessing it's about rooting out a spy. My money's on that Harrington chap." Ben winked. "Or is that too obvious?"

"Well, duh!" Kev snorted. "But it's hard to decide what to do next when we don't know the overall purpose."

"Did I not stress it?" Isaac smirked. "This scenario's all about *your* secret goals. There is no group objective."

Georgie frowned. "I know you said we wouldn't always be working as a team. But we don't even have a common goal? I'm not sure what to think about that. Kev's scenario was a bit unorthodox but even *he* didn't do that."

"I'm sure you'll figure it out." He ignored the frowns. "Look, if it helps, I'll keep track of how you're doing against your objectives, and if there's anything you're struggling with, you can always ask for a private session to work on stuff. Okay?" After a general assent he grinned. "I guessed you ladies would take the sexist attitudes path."

Jen didn't bite. "I found something which will blow you all away. It's taking a while to get my head around, but it'll certainly satisfy my main goal."

"You got more than one?" Georgie glared.

Isaac held up his hands. "I didn't want to overload you with all the grotty work stuff going on. I have a number of secondary missions for people who want more."

Jen stepped in. "And mine are linked - they both require me to go deep into the coding techniques."

"I'm with you on the needing to know more." Ben reached for another slice of garlic bread. "I've looked ahead a bit and I could do with a separate session to get to grips with the complicated decryption techniques."

Kev nodded. "Count me in. It's hard stuff."

An opportunity landed midweek when Georgie had a summons to watch the first UEFA quarter final at home. "Sorry, but it's Dad's birthday and his idea of a treat is the whole family watching a match together."

"Even if it's women playing?"

"Are you kidding? Any football is king. It's England – he's got a lot of affection for the Lionesses. You lot carry on without me because the technical stuff leaves me cold."

Kev suggested instead of running it as a session, they merely pooled all their research so far.

"That's not exactly in the spirit of the place." Isaac pouted. "It was all about compartmentalising everything."

"I get that, but we don't have access to the actual machines and the raw data, so it's not very satisfying."

"What stopped you downloading the simulator and having a play?"

Kev squirmed. "I did, but I couldn't get it to work. It just came out as gobbledegook."

"I'm not surprised. It's so complicated it took me five goes to get it right. There are so many opportunities to make a mistake and it doesn't help that the messages are all in German so you can't even tell if it's correct because so many of their words are gibberish anyway."

"Which one did you use? There's a stack of them." Ben flashed the list on his phone.

She perused it. "Can't see it." She showed them the site she'd used. "There's a video showing you how to do it using the actual monthly settings they would have used."

Kev peeked over her shoulder as she brought up a table on her screen. "Something like that kept coming up when I searched for Enigma codebook. I just about translated the German for plug links and ID groups, but couldn't figure the difference between roller position and ring position."

Ben joined in. "So this steckbrett I kept coming across is nothing to do with bread."

"What?"

"The translation is breadboard."

Isaac sniffed, turning it into a scoff. "That's what they used to call circuit boards before PCBs came along. They had a matrix of holes you could slot in components like resistors and capacitors to design your electrical device."

"All right, Professor Proton." Kev nudged his arm. "So what's this Steckerverbindungenin the fourth column?"

"It shows which pairs to connect on the plugboard. The top line has B to F, S to D and A to Y et cetera. But there's only ten pairs. So six letters won't be linked."

Kev blinked at her. "You've really done a number on this, haven't you?"

"You have no idea. I watched every episode of the *Bletchley Circle* – even the ones where the Miss Marples hang out in San Francisco."

"Yeah, I saw something about a French guy who had a German spy passing him stuff – they even got a couple of the machines." Kev grinned. "I wondered about the possibility of a Polish spy, but then I realised they'd done that storyline in the *Enigma* movie with Kate Winslett."

"Oohhh – the one with Jaime Lannister? I loved that."

Kev rolled his eyes at Jen. "So if they didn't have that codebook, how the heck could they work out all those settings? It beggars belief."

"That's where the cribs and Jeffreys sheets came in. You guess a phrase like 'Heil Hitler' and try all manner of different combinations until something stacks up. Even today it would take a computer a while to crack it."

Isaac had obviously foreseen this as he'd prepared a couple of short examples for them to try, talking them through the steps on the simulation tool and Jen was chuffed when she cracked the message several minutes ahead of the others. They then tried making up short messages and encoding them, first with the same settings, then with just one or two slight adjustments to the initial settings and seeing how drastically it changed the output.

"That's mental. I just moved the rotor setting by one letter and it's completely different." Kev wrote down the last letter and handed it to Ben. "See if you can get it."

At the end of the session, they all agreed that simply understanding how to operate the machines somehow helped them to get a handle on the whole thing.

"Good. Mission accomplished. I hope it serves you well in the next session." The gleam in Isaac's eye suggested they'd need all the help they could get.

Kev asked for a short private session to set up an essential task to achieve one of his goals, and it was sufficiently trivial that they fitted it in before Georgie returned from her dad's.

By Friday they were itching to have another go, leaving work early so they could eat the instant he came back and finish the session before the match started at eight.

Ben scrolled his phone. "Second-ranked Sweden against nineteenth Belgium – can't see it being much of a match, especially after Sweden annihilated Portugal five-nil."

"But they could be secret giant-killers." Kev checked the time. *Again*. "This waiting for His Maj is getting on my ti…wick."

"Good recovery." Jen grinned.

Kev grimaced. "It'll all be worth it when we finally get to stop being Sheldon's taxi service." The similarities between their landlord and the *Big Bang Theory* star hadn't lessened any in the past few years.

"Only if he manages not to annoy the examiner enough to pass." Ben deadpanned.

"And then there's the six-month investigation to ensure he's got the most energy-efficient – and cheapest – model."

"Aarrgghh. You know him so well." Ben winked at Georgie. "But he *is* your cousin."

Another grimace. "Whatever. Surely he could have his driving lesson on a different day."

"Did I not mention? My bad." Jen reached for a carrot and peeled it with exasperating nonchalance.

For the life of him, Kev couldn't wait her out. "Well?"

Her eyes sparkled. "Such an easy mark. Never play poker, Kev. You're way too easy to wind up. I reckon he only wants us to *believe* he's having driving lessons."

He frowned. "What do you know?"

"Only that I spotted him getting into a red U-Drive car after the launch party – because he wanted me to."

"Explain."

"Since the start, if anyone asked him what he did on Friday, he'd just do that Mona Lisa smile–"

"The one that says 'it's for me to know and you to find out'?" Ben rolled his eyes.

"Unless he's actually saying the words." Kev snorted.

"Or tapping the side of his nose as though directing you where to land a punch." Georgie ground her teeth.

Kev chuckled. "I thought it was only me."

"We've all been there, trust me." Jen resumed her tale, recounting his "accidental" spilling of prosecco as an excuse to leave the party. "I didn't realise at the time, but his suspicious manner was designed to make me take note. And if he was trying to keep it a secret, why have the instructor pick him up in view of the office?"

Ben narrowed his eyes. "I never twigged at the time, but there was a copy of the Highway Code on his desk."

"Sounds like he wanted us to know." Kev shrugged.

"So why not mention it? You know him – if he could get one of us to give him free lessons …" Ben gestured.

"True. You're gonna have to clue us in, Jen."

"You'd think, if he's genuinely getting driving lessons, one of us would have spotted him being dropped off by now. I reckon it's just a cover and he's actually got a secret project on he doesn't want us to figure out."

"Something to do with the time capsule, you mean?" Kev threw it out and, sure enough, the other three couldn't disguise the unease in their swapped glances. "You lot must think I came down with yesterday's rain. Trying to fob me off with red herrings when all the while you've been scheming and plotting with him–"

"That's not true." Georgie protested. "Ben and I did it by accident, and Isaac tricked Jen into–"

"What the fuck?" Kev jumped up. "Are you trying to tell me you lot have actually …?" He peered at them shaking his head. "Nah, this is a wind up, isn't it? You're just mucking with my head."

Jen stood. "There's only one way to convince you." She dashed out of the room and up the stairs.

The others followed suit and they reached the door to the attic panting. Jen tried it – locked.

From the inside because the key filled the keyhole.

Undeterred, she produced a hair grip and fiddled around until a small thud said it had dropped out.

"Aren't you supposed to slide a newspaper under to catch it or something?"

"Bless you, Georgie. That's so-oo Famous Five." With a grin, Ben produced another key and unlocked it.

They piled in and barely had time to assure Kev no one was hiding in the bathroom when Isaac materialised, landing on the floor with a thump.

Ch 4 – Kev's Turn

July 2022

*"What the actual **Fuck**?* Sorry, ladies." As Kev again forgot to clean up his language, the others galvanised into action around Isaac, who squirmed on the floor, clutching his guts and groaning.

"What happened? Have you been hurt?" Georgie tried to move his arms to reveal more clues.

As he retched, Jen dashed over to the kitchenette, returning with the orange bowl from under the sink, crossing paths with Ben, who'd fetched a glass of water.

Isaac downed it in three gulps and held out the empty glass with a whispered, "Please."

His frown deepening, Kev watched the others minister like well-co-ordinated paramedics until Isaac had recovered enough to sit on the futon sipping hot, sweet tea and nibbling a banana.

Kev's patience, already extended way beyond his natural tolerance, passed its sell-by. "Is someone going to explain before my head implodes?"

Ben did the honours. "Isaac's suffering the after-effects of a time-travel journey. Or jaunt sounds better."

As the others nodded agreement, Kev frowned, "And you lot know exactly what to do because …?

"We've all travelled into the past." Georgie grimaced. "More than once for Ben and I. Every jaunt takes a toll, although some of us are more badly affected than others."

"I bloody knew it. You've all gone bonkers. Nuts." A head-shake. "Way too much sci-fi on TV."

Jen tutted. "So how do you explain what you just saw?"

He floundered for an explanation, then folded his arms. "Smoke and mirrors. Bloody clever ones, admittedly."

Another tut. "Exactly how do–"

Isaac's coughing fit cut Jen off, and she relieved him of the mug before he got a lapful of scalding tea.

Despite the convenient timing, the violent hacking wasn't fake; Isaac's eyes bulged with the effort. He calmed enough for another couple of sips before croaking out an apology. "Sorry, Kev. It's all true. No smoke; no mirrors. I didn't want to tell anyone until I'd tested it thoroughly."

"With unsuspecting human guinea pigs?" Jen's tone accused.

"Even more sorry. I wasn't sure you'd agree."

"That's no kind of excuse. And you don't know me very well if you think that."

"Actually, it's not true at all; I've witnessed your courage many times. I've no idea why I thought that."

"Because you're a rotten stinking liar?"

Everyone recoiled at Georgie's vehemence.

Isaac shook his head. "You're absolutely right. Please forgive me, Georgie." He shrugged. "When Ben released the dice accidently I didn't fully understand the mechanism. And then Jen dropped the dice–"

"Wait – you dropped the dice too?" Ben frowned. "What are the chances?"

"A lot lower than you might think because of muscle memory. What else do you do with dice but roll them?"

"Yeah, but dropping and throwing are very different–"

"Not to the dice." Isaac smirked. "However, you're on

the right lines. When *you* dropped them, because of your connection to the seventies, they both landed on seven. I presume you ended in 1977?"

"I *knew* you knew." Georgie glared at him. "Why haven't you mentioned it before?"

He held her gaze. "I could ask *you* the same."

"Because we didn't trust you." After Jen blurted it out, everyone in the room stilled.

Georgie backed her up. "Even before the whole false-fiancé thing."

The atmosphere disrupted to tornado-aftermath levels, the brunt led by Kev. "And there was me thinking I knew you all." He glared at Ben. "There's a decade's worth of loyalty, right there. Or not."

"Sorry, mate. There's no excuse for it."

"Damn right there isn't." His lip twitched. "A guy could get seriously paranoid living with you bloody bunch."

"Can we skip the part where everyone gets stressed about stuff we can't change and focus on the good bits?" Isaac's expression was serious red-rag-bull material.

Especially to Georgie. "Just because you don't have as much emotional intelligence as your tea mug doesn't mean the rest of us can shake it off in a heartbeat."

Kev recognised the signs. "One day, Pet, you'll tell me exactly what he did when you guys were young. *I* got over myself about the secret-keeping a while ago." It had been a long, hard struggle, but Kev had learnt to control his vicious temper, and knew how much humour helped. He prayed it would be the same for her. "I know it's no substitute for a good rant, but …" Before she could protest, he pulled her up from her perch and swamped her in a squeezy bear-hug until she succumbed with a giggle.

Ben took the lead in describing his and Georgie's jaunt to meet Isaac's grandparents during the Queen's silver jubilee, joining in a street party the day after her platinum celebration. When he spoke about their return detouring via an alternate 2022, Isaac paled.

"What? I didn't realise that could happen."

Georgie scoffed. "Seriously? In all your trips you've never ended up somewhere else?"

He paused, eyes sliding downwards.

"No more secrets or lies, please. This is important."

His head jerked up and he maintained a steady gaze as he described a jaunt which ended in grey nothingness.

"Like some kind of limbo?" Ben raised an eyebrow.

"Exactly. Oh dear. Maybe we should've had some kind of debrief when you two got back. But I was so wrapped up in … never mind." An eye dart. "Tell me more about this alternate place. Like what made it different."

Georgie wasn't pulling any punches. "The fact you and Kev were misogynistic chavs was a massive giveaway." She sniggered. "And Jen went all Stepford wives, simpering when you smacked her bum."

"Now that I'd have paid to see." Kev grinned, earning a slap from Jen.

She slid a glance. "From what they said, I wouldn't have noticed any difference in you."

"Ouch. Kick a guy when he's down, why don't you?"

"Anything else?" Isaac brought them back on task. "What about the setting?"

"The house was more like when your nan lived there. We stayed in the house, so we've no idea what it was like outside."

"Right. Maybe you could both do a report—"

"You mean like something written?" Georgie frowned.

"A voice note will do. Just describe anything you can remember, especially about the jaunts."

"Don't hold your breath. I've forgotten a lot of the detail. Now if you'd suggested it a month ago …"

"All right. Maybe the three of us could sit down and I'll work up some questions based on Eric's observations."

"You've cracked the code?" Kev perked up.

"One of the early ones. It was just a simple Caesar shift. But it didn't give me much."

"How cool would it be if the Bletchley scenario gave us decryption skills so we could crack the notebook?"

"The way playing a monk made you a badass fighter?" Ben chucked as Kev responded with a raised middle finger.

"But all the research is helping. Most of what's in Grampy's notebook is inaccessible, and the more I learn, the more I realise that the majority of the codes he used are impossible unless you know which method."

"Not forgetting having the key to unlock it."

"Exactly. Now we're all on the same page and know a bit more about decryption techniques, we can work together. I'm hoping the more we practice, the better we'll get at recognising the different methods."

Kev grunted. "Best of luck with that. I don't have anything like the patience you need to do those Jeffreys sheets. But the Enigma app was fun."

"Except where would Eric get hold of an Enigma machine?" Jen had obviously thought about this. "They surely wouldn't have had that app back in the nineties."

"No. But he did have a time-capsule, don't forget." Isaac grinned. "And he visited Bletchley Park regularly when they opened it as a museum."

Kev changed the subject. "So what happened to you, Jen? I'll take a wild guess you ended up in the fifties."

"Yep. And I got to hang out with my gran Vickie."

"The one who played tennis at Wimbledon?" A face-palm. "Of course. You were there during the tournament. Not in this year's, but seventy years earlier. Cool."

"Totally. I didn't see her play properly, but I watched her in a knock-about with that year's junior champions."

"And you didn't have a problem with everything being so … different?"

"Not as much as you might imagine. Apart from the lack of cars and technology–"

"Not to mention the cutesy fashions." He winked.

She gestured at her outfit. "Really not so different. Everyone spoke properly, enunciating consonants."

"Like an old black and white movie?"

"Precisely. Even the Yanks sounded more like RP."

"You mean received pronunciation. Proper posh, like the Queen speaks." Georgie got in a second before Kev.

"Yanks? That's not very woke."

Jen blushed. "It's how Vickie – my gran – referred to them. And that's the second time someone's called me woke. Is that how I come across?" Her lip wobbled.

"Not to most people." Georgie jumped in quickly. "Just

the Neanderthals." She glared at Kev and Isaac.

"Anyway, Isaac did an awful lot of preparation, buying a suitable suitcase, filling it with clothes from the rack and even booking a room in my great gran's B&B. Some of this was useful, but it would have helped if I'd known."

"As I said, I would've told you, but the timing went pear-shaped. I didn't spot they'd moved the tournament, so I had to follow and settle you on the park bench."

"So you made a number of journeys to set this all up." Kev's scrutiny made Isaac squirm. "Did no-one see you? Surely you've seen or read enough to know the potential problems with meddling in the past."

"I minimised it with careful planning." A smirk.

"But not clever enough. Your stalking Vickie had real effect on her mental health. They were both anxious because that kind of behaviour was unknown in 1955."

"Hang on a sec. I'm seeing a pattern here." Kev wrote down the dates of both jaunts. "It seems the time travel works when you throw a double number – is that right?

Several nods.

"We figured it was linked to master numbers." Ben offered. "You know, eleven, twenty-two, thirty-three."

"Aka double numbers." Kev scoffed. "And I would suggest you can only go back to the same day on that year."

"All my findings to date concur. That's why it's been a pig to plan anything."

"Except I jumped back three days from the 30th to the 27th." Jen tapped on the page.

"A glitch. Never happened before."

"Given that everyone else has had a go, I reckon it has

to be my turn." Kev challenged, but no one denied.

"I'm so sorry, mate. Normally I'd have scouted it out and got an idea of the lay of the land, but I think I need to back off."

"No kidding." Georgie glared at him. "You have no idea what all this mucking with the timeline is doing to your body, but the evidence suggests it's nothing good."

"A bit of a runny nose never killed anyone." He sniffed.

"Mate, you're in a really bad way." Ben gasped his shoulder. "We noticed the effects on our bodies after a few jaunts, but it sounds like you've done dozens."

He shrugged. "The nausea and headaches get worse if I do too many, too close together."

"No kidding. I suffered even on the first time."

"Probably because you're such a nature girl."

"True." Georgie grinned. "I don't think you should go alone, Kev. It's a lot easier if there are two of you."

Isaac nodded. "And a lot safer because you'll each have your own set of dice." He explained how each pair imprinted on the first person to use them. "If my theory holds true, you'll end up in 1988, so you'll need a suitable cover story."

"Which won't be a problem if I go with you. We can use the distant relative thing again."

"He may remember you from seventy-seven."

"Even better. I'll use the same name."

"But you won't look eleven years older."

"Are you kidding? I don't look a day older than I did at twenty-one. And anyway, I'll be dressed differently."

Kev jumped up. "Come on then. Let's suit up."

Jen groaned. "Only you, mate. Only you."

"If you knew how long I've waited to use that line …"

"Trust me, mate. We know." Ben grinned.

"Just a moment. There's a stack of important information you need to know about time travel."

"Don't worry I'll wing it. You didn't tell any of the others. Or are you saying I'm too dumb to work it out?"

"Actually, there's a whole bunch of stuff Ben and I wish we'd known before we went, and Jen had Isaac looking after her. Sit down and listen." Georgie pulled his arm.

With a grudging glare, he listened while the three of them made suggestions based on their experiences, most of which was common sense, but Ben's advice about keeping schtum and batting back questions sounded golden. As did the back-pack with water and a first-aid kit.

Jen explained about the L-shaped carriage-return, line-feed symbol for returning to the present. She glanced at Isaac. "Or is it just back to the previous jaunt?"

He shrugged. "Your guess is as good as mine. I've only ever gone to my intended destination and returned here. Apart from the limbo trip, when I returned without rolling. It was right at the start when I didn't know much about anything, and I was so shaken up I nearly gave it all up."

Her tone softened. "It must have been scary."

"And then some. I really wanted to involve you guys, but I couldn't risk putting you in danger." A shrug. "So many things could have gone wrong." He muttered something which sounded like "And did."

"Like what?" Kev narrowed his eyes.

"It's all to do with the numbers. Eric has somehow put

in a safeguard so it won't trigger except on a double. As you said, the energy of a master number is extremely powerful, making a strong connection."

"Is it to do with resonant frequencies?"

"Exactly. So as you've all spotted, we each have a preferred decade which resonates most, making it easier to jaunt. And travelling on the same date strengthens the connection, too."

"So you're saying it's safest to go to 22nd July 1988. Hey, there's another master number – should be a breeze."

Famous last words.

After all the excitement of gathering the essentials in a backpack and changing into 80s gear, Kev sat on the floor of the time capsule trying a few calming breaths. The others had moved to Isaac's room, and he heard their exclamations of the set-up he'd used to monitor the jaunts.

Isaac's disembodied voice suggested he cleared his mind and focussed on the numbers he wanted to throw.

"A six and seven, right?" Kev chuckled.

"It's no joke. Because that's only one digit away from sixty-six, you could end up there. Hold on a second."

Georgie took his hands. "Honestly, you should listen. I know you're nervous and excited, but Ben made a similar comment and the dice landed on the numbers he mentioned. It's quite spooky really."

"Okay, try now."

Kev threw them, unsurprised when they landed on six and seven. "Okay, guys, point taken. I need eighty-eight, so I'm looking for an eight and another eight."

"Maybe don't throw so hard because they roll so far."

This time he blew on them first, and the gentle roll gave a seven and nine. He grunted. "Getting closer – only a year off the eighties. In the famous words of a pale serpent: *Here I Go Again*."

"Whitesnake." Georgie's grin dimmed slightly. "I just remembered. When they stop rolling, pick them up straight away because the transfer happens quite fast. Also, we held hands after the time Ben went into limbo."

The third go gave six and five, and when Kev opened his mouth, she put a finger over it. "Don't say it. Or even think about it. Sorry. It was probably too many instructions and your brain couldn't focus."

"Why not try dropping them instead of throwing?" Isaac's suggestion made sense, but Kev didn't give any preparation and the resulting five and nine couldn't have been further apart.

"Sorry, I should have been clearer. Just let them fall, and take your time."

He grinned. "Maybe I gotta have *Faith*?"

She couldn't resist. "*Don't Stop Believing*."

Except the computer had other ideas, giving her three-minute warning about the door sealing.

"What happened to the ten-minute one?" Kev grumbled. "Not sure if it's even worth doing this." Before Georgie could speak he opened his fingers and the two dice fell the short distance and tumbled to a stop.

All the lights cut out except a red flashing bulb, accompanied by a loud klaxon. "Warning. Number of attempts exceeded. Evacuate now."

Ch 5 – Football Crazy

July 2022

Kev scrambled to his feet, pulling Georgie with him, but when he reached the keypad, he couldn't remember the number. Thankfully, she could and tapped in $1 - 3 - 8 - 8$.

Nothing happened.

"Isaac. Did you change the code?"

The panic in her voice fired Kev's already sky-high blood pressure and adrenalin spikes crawled through the muscles in his back and neck.

A burst of static scrambled any chance of hearing his reply, and he groaned.

"Hang on. Shhh."

He listened. The static repeated in a rhythm.

"Dash-dash-dash. O. Dash-dot. N. Dash-dash-dash. He's saying no."

"So what do we do?"

"Trust. Have some patience."

"That's easy for you to say. You totally get Zen."

"Sometimes. My gut's telling me all will be well."

Kev farted – not quite silent, but utterly deadly. "Sorry. My gut has other ideas. Something else to add to the preparation list. Ensure bowel–"

"There you go. Panic over." Georgie pointed at the keypad as it glowed green and a door-sized amount of wall surrounding it moved towards them.

"'Bout bloody time." Kev gestured for her to go first.

Ben waited outside the door, trying to hide his anxiety and Jen scooped Georgie into her arms.

"That was a close one." Ben jumped back as the door closed. "I take it you didn't get a full house."

Kev had clenched the dice tightly in his left hand to preserve the score, and he placed them on the shelf where the nine and seven mocked him. "One off the eight both times. Just my luck."

"Never mind, mate. You can have another go tomorrow. At least, I assume you can."

"How come you didn't tell us about the maximum number of attempts?" Georgie attacked Isaac the second he walked into the attic.

"Because I didn't know. I've always jaunted on the first or second go. Possibly because I'd done more preparation and knew exactly when and where I wanted to go."

"And how come the smug git didn't warn me when I only had one throw left?" Kev glared. "The sooner we get that notebook decrypted the better."

"More worrying, why has it stopped giving the ten-minute warning?" Ben wandered over to the keypad, now flashing red, and read the scrolling LCD message. "She's gone in a huff and not playing for the next twenty hours." He frowned. "Not the normal twenty-four while she decontaminates from contact with dusty humans."

As though in response, a low-frequency humming indicated the capsule's pumps were evacuating all the air from the chamber to eliminate the dust particles.

"Tharr she blows." Kev chuckled. "Although methinks a tad delayed. Like the door opening."

Isaac shrugged. "Each jaunt – or attempted jaunt, apparently – seems to take it out of her. I suggest this is the reason for the limit of four."

Kev swapped a knowing glance with Georgie. A few weeks ago, Isaac had berated them for personifying the computer as a female. But he'd taken it a step further, suggesting she could be exhausted.

The following morning saw them all in the "office," delving deeper into the mysteries of Eric's notebook. Now they knew more about the Enigma code, Isaac identified a couple of sections where the pages were filled with groups of five letters. "At least we have the advantage that it won't be in German. I suggest we use the rodding technique with a few crib phrases like 'dice,' 'year' and 'double.' If anyone thinks of likely cribs, do share them."

After the sixth attempt proved as fruitless as the first five, Kev shoved the book across the desk and it fell down the back.

"Temper, temper." Jen winked, knowing full well how much that phrase wound him up.

"It's useless without knowing something about the settings. We're on a hiding to nothing."

"Got somewhere better to be?" Georgie grinned.

"Yes. Nineteen eighty eight."

"Not for another–" Isaac consulted his watch and grinned. "Eighty eight minutes. I recommend you try to keep your brain occupied between now and then or it will stress to the point where you can't hope to make a connection."

Kev scrabbled under the desk for the notebook, banging his head as he came back up. It triggered an idea and he called over to Isaac. "I don't suppose you still have Grampy Eric's old desk somewhere? I bet it had a secret panel somewhere and we'd find a list with all the keys to the codes. He must have written them down somewhere separate from the notebook."

"One of my first thoughts. But he must have ditched it when he got the modern ones in the capsule. The synthetic laminates collect less dust and are easier to wipe clean."

Kev folded his arms. "I can't think of anything more stressful than this futile exercise. It's a total waste of time. Chocolate teapot useless."

Jen shook her head. "There is something useful you could do, but it's pretty mindless."

"Should suit me then. Mindless I can do."

"It involves typing in each page. When we *do* discover the key, as I'm confident we will, we'll have all the source material so we can easily copy and paste it into the app. It'll take hours off the whole thing."

He scoffed. "Sod that for a game of soldiers. I can just scan it in with OCR."

She slid a glance. "Go for it."

He downloaded an optical character recognition app and captured the first three pages.

"Before you go much further, you might want to check it against the original."

He did as she suggested, snorting in disgust. "Five errors in the first three lines. That's about as useful as an inflatable dartboard. You could've told me."

An eye roll. "Would you have listened?"

"'Nuff said. So which is quicker?

"Six of one and half-a-dozen of the other. You could try a page each way and decide which you prefer."

He did as instructed, but it got old very quickly.

Jen took pity. "Now you have it electronically, it's a lot easier to check it's not a straight Caesar shift."

"I thought Isaac would have done that."

"He did a few, but didn't make a note of the failures."

"Are we talking ashtray-on-a-motorbike useful?"

She chuckled. "Or even roll-on hairspray."

It took a beat, then he laughed out loud. "That's a new one. I'm stealing it for my collection."

Using Jen's trick, Kev dived deep into the rabbit hole, so when Ben tapped his watch, he held up a hand. "Gimme five – I'm onto something here."

When it didn't come out in five minutes, he tore himself away reluctantly, and Isaac suggested a ten-minute meditation to clear his mind.

This time needed much less preparation, and Georgie was already wearing an 80's shirt and denim dungaree shorts. Some oversize hooped earrings and black lace fingerless gloves with a matching bow in her hair completed the look.

"You'd better take a jacket – I looked up the weather and there was a lot of rain that weekend, although the temperature was comfortable."

Isaac quirked a lip. "I'm impressed. Every bit of research you do like that improves your connection to the time and place. Fingers crossed."

But it was no better. Despite his attempts to focus only on eights. Kev rolled 76, 69 and 56. Pausing, he raised an eyebrow at Georgie, but she shook her head.

"Sorry, mate. I've not done it, so I don't have a clue."

Helpfully, the computer gave a warning this time. "You have one attempt left."

"You couldn't have mentioned this yesterday?" He had no control over the snarky Jewish accent.

"I can only operate in the present day."

A snort. "That's me told." He stared up at the camera. "Any advice Obi-Wan?"

Nothing.

Then Ben's voice. "He means you."

An exasperated tut. "I know that, I'm not stupid. I was merely trying to think of what worked for me. Maybe Georgie can help. Are you thinking of eights too?"

She glared at the camera. "Of course I am. Not just thinking but visualising eighty-eight in my head."

"That's a good idea. Try that, Kevin."

Clearing his mind, he closed his eyes, picturing two fat party balloons in the shape of eights. Bringing the dice to his lips, he kissed each one and let go, not daring to look.

Georgie squeezed his arm. "Sorry. Nine and six. We should leave pronto."

"Just a tick." Kev retrieved his flash drive from the USB port Isaac had wired up to one of the external serial ports.

"What's that for?"

"A hunch. Don't want to explain in case I'm wrong."

"No spoilers, then. But what if you need help?"

"I'll ask."

They exited to find the others back in the attic, and Kev read out the scrolling message announcing no more attempts for at least three days. "And woe betide anyone who dares to try." He winked.

"Surely it doesn't say that." Georgie's gullibility knew no bounds.

"Of course not. He's just pulling your leg." Isaac scoffed. "But she will need some recovery time."

"What's with all the personification?" Kev slapped his back. "You jumped down our throats a few weeks ago for doing the same."

"If you can't beat them ..." He shrugged. "And anyway, I feel rude calling her an it."

"Seriously guys. Have you never watched AI movies?" Jen shook her head.

"Yeah, but it's no Cyberdyne, let alone Ultron."

Ben deadpanned. "I'd say more like Aida."

"From *Agents of S.H.I.E.L.D.*? Are you saying there's an LMD in Isaac's wardrobe?" Kev nudged his arm. "You sly old dog, you."

"Enough with the pop-culture references. I bugged out on that series when we lost Grant Ward." Georgie pouted.

While they teased, Jen had drawn a grid on the whiteboard with all the combinations of five to nine. She'd colour coded Kev's numbers from the two days. She folded her arms. "Thought so. What do you notice?"

	5	6	7	8	9
5	55	56	57	58	59
6	65	66	67	68	69
7	75	76	77	78	79
8	85	86	87	88	89
9	95	96	97	98	99

As Kev studied the grid, he quickly spotted what she was getting at. "Not a single eight."

"Looks like the universe is trying to tell you something, mate. Or at least the time capsule is." Ben chuckled.

"Here's the second bunch of numbers." Jen wrote them out below the grid. 76, 69, 56, 96. "Notice anything?"

Georgie was first. "They all have a six somewhere."

"Not only that. Every number adjacent to sixty-six came up." Isaac pointed to them. "Hmmm. I wonder if you could have influenced it in some way. I've not studied the effect of a second person in the chamber."

"Her presence didn't stop me getting two sevens." Ben reminded. "Twice."

While they waited for the last quarter final to start, Jen declared she'd seen more than enough pre-football coverage to last her a lifetime. "I'm not that interested in re-runs of the Netherland's best bits or learning that a French player's father played in a previous World Cup. Certainly not enough to spend the next couple of hours."

Georgie scrolled through the channels, stopping on an extended news feature showing highlights of the week's baton relay for the up-and-coming Commonwealth Games.

"Not this again." Kev groused. "I'm fed up hearing about the four thousand mile journey across a hundred and eighty countries."

"It's two-and-a-half thousand miles and seventy-two countries." Georgie rolled her eyes.

"Whatever. It didn't come anywhere near us and I don't care about any of these little Midland villages."

"That's mean. It was in Warwick yesterday." As

Georgie spoke, footage of a castle came up.

"Blimey – it didn't look that bashed in when we visited it." Ben quipped.

"It's Kenilworth – but you know that." Jen groaned.

"So is this gonna be like the jubilee with hours of the same sad acts dragged out to sing the same old songs?"

"Actually it's mostly Brummie acts – Dad reckons it's the home of decent rock. Sabbath, Judas Priest and ELO."

Isaac sniffed. "How about UB40, Dexys and The Beat?"

"Didn't know you were into all that Ska stuff."

"It's up to you if you want to miss the opening ceremony, but I'll probably watch it." Jen folded her arms.

"And Georgie definitely will – she's proper patriotic."

"Actually, I may not bother." She slid an enigmatic grin.

The match was pretty much a washout. France dominated, with a dozen shots on target but were unable to score until an extra time penalty. Georgie went to bed early, claiming an early start the next day. She left before the rest of them surfaced and stayed out till Monday evening, when she refused to discuss her whereabouts.

Tuesday's semi-final saw Sweden on top form at the beginning, with a goal attempt in the first minute and constant pressure even after Beth Mead's goal at thirty-four minutes.

The gang got fresh beers for the second half, cheering as Mead returned the compliment to Lucy Bronze, setting her up to head in the second goal. Something magical happened as Russo, fresh from the bench, kept the Swedish goalie busy with two failed attempts, followed by an outrageous back heel which shot through Lindahl's legs. Everyone shot out of their seats, dancing around the room. Amid the ensuing "they think it's all over" celebrations, they nearly missed Kirby's cheeky chip over Lindahl's head for a fourth goal.

Kev felt honour-bound to quip, "it is now."

"That's poetic justice, right there." Isaac offered.

"Because the Lionesses just handed the top team their butts after they slaughtered Portugal?" Kev grinned. "Or because Kirby and Lindahl both played for Chelsea?"

"Get you with knowing about the women players." Jen and Georgie clinked their bottles of Bud.

"As if. The commentator just said it, but you two were too busy doing a victory dance. There's still fifteen minutes to go, you know. Not to jinx it or anything."

On Wednesday, in the ninety minutes before the second semi-final started, they brought Georgie up to speed on some of the other coding techniques, such as the Vigenère cipher, which used a square grid with the alphabet forming the rows and columns, offset by one letter each time. Ben took her through step-by-step, encoding and decoding simple examples until she grasped it and then created a longer message. It was painstaking, time-consuming work, but well worth the effort when she decoded it on her own.

Kev brought up the site Jen had found which took the hard work out of the decryption, and they each tried a different page in Eric's notebook using Isaac's best-guess suggestions for potential keys.

"If you have a Vigenère grid, I've discovered a way to

speed things up." Beckoning him over, she demonstrated how to pick a three-letter coded word and align the three search boxes vertically with the clue letters at the top of each column. "You just go down a row at a time and write down anything which looks like it could be a word – or part of a word. I use an envelope to make it easier to spot."

"Pretty cool, Jen. You're damn good at this stuff."

"Not quite good enough. That site gives details of a method to crack it by guessing the key length and subtracting the ciphertext from itself, offset by that length."

He face-palmed. "*Duh*. So obvious."

A grin. "Perzackly. But it's excruciatingly tedious. I thought about automating it, but it's way low priority."

After the previous evening's thrilling match, the gang were expecting the most successful nation in European women's football history to dispatch France with typical German efficiency. The French team managed to stave off the inevitable for half an hour of the second half before their defeat at the hands – or even feet – of Popp.

"That's it then. An England–Germany final, just like 1966." Every ensuing report picked up on this as the media went on a feeding frenzy as frantic as any pride of lions.

When Thursday came, Georgie finally admitted where she'd dashed off to on the Sunday. One of the girls performing had given her an invitation to attend the opening ceremony rehearsal. "It was pretty mind-blowing."

"Now we *have* to watch it." Kev resisted grumpily, but in the end was every bit as absorbed as the rest when Georgie played back her recording. Yet again, the country's best and brightest joined together at Alexander Stadium to showcase what the commentator called the "vivid and vibrant confidence" of Birmingham.

Lenny Henry had been involved in one of the last stages of the baton relay, and the opening video showed athletes packing their shards of light which represented fragments of the Commonwealth stars. A convoy of red, white and blue cars paid tribute to the car-manufacturing heritage, and Prince Charles joined in, driving a blue Aston Martin.

As each new section of the clever storyline unfolded, Kev asked if Georgie's friend was in this bit, but she merely smiled. The undoubted star of the show was a ten-metre-high mechanical bull, which provided a catalyst for the female chain-makers of the Industrial Revolution to break free. The most moving part was when a couple of aerial artists spiralled down to remove the mask subjugating the bull, and they were all enthralled.

Georgie sat back, wiping away a tear. "That's Lindsey. How brilliant is she?"

"*That's* your friend?" Kev choked on his words. "Stunning. Just stunning. No one's gonna forget those two in a hurry."

"How did she get the gig?" Ben seemed equally impressed. "This isn't her first rodeo."

"Nope. She's been doing the aerial stuff for several years now. The other girl is the class teacher."

When the parade of the athletes from the seventy-two participating nations began, Kev led the boys' grumbles. "We don't have to watch this bit do we?"

"Only if you want to." Georgie skipped to the closing

act – Duran Duran. Kitted out in Day-Glo colours, the band reminded people why they were so popular in the eighties. A cast of thousands partied with them, accompanied by spectacular visuals with doves, psychedelic colours and thousands of phone torches.

"I know what to get for your next birthday, Kev." Ben chuckled as the camera focussed on Nick Rhodes bopping away on his keyboard.

"I can just see you in buttercup yellow and fuchsia pink." Georgie slid a glance.

"Whaddya mean? I lent him that suit." Kev pointed at the screen. "And the matching shades."

"Yeah, but it's so much groovier with his white hair. And he's even got matching boots. Classy." Jen grinned.

The set ended with the inevitable firework display, and Kev was amused how it no longer had the power to hold their attention. "Any other year we'd be glued to the screen, saying things like 'phenomenal.' But this is the – what – fourth display in mere weeks?"

"Something like that. It's been a helluva year."

"And it's only half over."

By Friday, Kev had done enough digging into the whole time-travel thing to realise none of it was accidental. Although not by conscious design, Ben's journey into the seventies was a direct result of a conversation with his grandparents about the silver jubilee and very much influenced by Georgie's preoccupation with the platinum one. Likewise with Jen and Wimbledon.

Although he hadn't explained them in any great detail,

Isaac's theories about the connection being strengthened by the power of thought felt compelling. And he couldn't rid himself of the image of sixty-six, surrounded by four of the numbers he'd rolled. The universe was definitely trying to tell him something. And the fact tomorrow was the exact date – albeit fifty-six years on – that England had beaten Germany made it a total no-brainer. Despite his assertion, it *wasn't* his turn – Georgie was the obvious candidate.

Her reaction was everything he could have wished for. "I did wonder. If it's true, you must come with me."

Isaac approved whole-heartedly. "Given the weight of evidence, sixty-six does make a lot more sense. However, I would suggest a change of venue." He glanced at her. "Do you remember telling me about your dad's entry into the world?"

She scoffed. "How could I forget? It's folk-lore in my family. Or is it legend? I never know the difference."

"Not important."

"No. Anyway, Dad was born on the day of the final and Gran was gutted she didn't get to watch the match, but it meant Grandad had a spare ticket."

"Really? You mean I could–"

"Prime directive. You can't change the past."

Ignoring Isaac's smug interjection, she continued. "He ended up taking one of Gran's cousins who'd turned up the night before with his wife."

Kev's face fell. "Oh. Hopes dashed much?"

Ben narrowed his eyes. "This sounds familiar. Do you know who it was?"

"That's the legendary part. He was a virtual stranger,

and no one can remember his name."

"Tell me he was never seen again. It sounds promising."

She shrugged. "Stranger things, Kev. Stranger things."

Shooting a withering glare, Isaac gave a few clues he'd picked up about travelling somewhere other than the same destination, and they made a few adjustments to the useful items, packing them into a handbag and knapsack from the 60s rack in the capsule.

With crazy attention to detail, Isaac showed them a historic weather site so they could select appropriate clothes to wear and pack. He suggested using the same vintage suitcase and rocking up a suitable backstory so they wouldn't get caught out.

"That's it then. We've covered every base. It *will* work this time, I feel it in my bones."

Ch 6 – Kenneth and Joy

Georgie had no doubt it would work; she'd been dreaming of her gran's house in Harlesden for several weeks. It started when Beth Mead's hat trick against Norway secured England a place in the Euro quarter finals. The commentator remarked it was her third hat-trick this season, and the three-by-three triggered something in Georgie's head. For several subsequent days the media buzzed about Geoff Hurst's hat trick against Germany all those years ago. *In 1966.*

From that point on, every journey saw at least half-a dozen sixty-six number plates – unheard of in an area where the vast majority of cars were less than three years old and it was rare to see plates other than 20s (or 70s of course) with the occasional 19 or 69.

When Kev rolled 67 and 65 on his first go, it took everything she had not to mention these were 66 ± 1, then the second go brought 56 and 76, i.e. 66 ± 10. The plus-or-minus symbols had appeared in her head, confirming the notion she was hanging around mathematically-minded geeks far too much; she'd even started thinking like them.

But she didn't want to voice the idea her energy might be affecting Kev's dice, and was glad she'd kept quiet when Ben pointed out how her presence hadn't affected his throws. Somewhere, in the back of her brain, a couple of neurons were poised on the edge, desperate to take the leap and make a connection, but they hesitated. *More data required, as Isaac would say.*

She'd agreed wholeheartedly when Kev said it was his turn, but when *she* rolled, the dice had barely left her hand before a shivery rush of goosebumps verified it was actually hers. Swiping the dice the instant they landed on double six, she grabbed Kev's arm with her other hand.

They landed in the park which Google Earth showed had barely changed since she'd played there as a kid – and possibly since Victorian times. Although still daylight, the rain had kept people away in droves.

"Let's hope Isaac's right and it is just a shower." She raised her umbrella.

Kev pulled up the collar on his mackintosh and set the hat at a slight angle. "Trust Isaac to know the difference between a fedora and a trilby. Does it look as good as I imagine?"

"Better." A grin. "Proper film-noir gumshoe."

"Yesss." He dropped a fist-pump. "Seeing as how you've done this before, and they're your folks I'm gonna leave all the talking to you."

"Going to."

"What?"

"If you'd invested half an hour watching Patrick Troughton's *Doctor Who*, you would know. Enunciate clearly and no slang."

"Why certainly, Mistress Georgiana." A deep bow.

"Prat. Wrong century. And try to remember we decided on Joy and Kenneth because you're bound to forget and they start with similar sounds."

"And we're supposed to be married right?"

"Because they wouldn't stand for anything else." She

twisted the ring.

"That twisting marks you out as a newlywed, and we're far too old for that."

"Now you're getting the hang of it."

The rain proved to be the perfect facilitator to smooth their entry into her gran's house. Along with the inconvenience of an extremely large belly, which encouraged the poor woman not to hang around on the doorstep asking questions.

Five minutes later, credentials established, they were sitting in the kitchen while her gran directed Georgie to the necessary paraphernalia for making a brew. Except she already knew from visits in the past – or in this case, the future. When she automatically went to the right cupboard – for the ubiquitous fruit cake – her gran commented.

"How curious you seem to know where everything is. Are you psychic?"

Oops. "Not at all. Your kitchen is so well laid out. My gran's used to be very similar."

Kev covered his sharp intake of breath by clearing his throat. "Where's your husband, Mrs T?"

"Polly, please. It's actually Pauline, but everyone calls me Pol. I like it – much friendlier."

"It suits you. Bright and cheerful."

"Aww, what a charmer you are Kenneth."

"Ken, please. Much friendlier."

She giggled. "And witty, too. You must be very pleased, love. I bet he has you in stitches, joking around."

"He does love a practical joke." Rolling her eyes, Georgie brought over the tray with the zany black-and-white tea-set she remembered so well.

Kev picked up a saucer, examining the dated images of a chair, houseplant, lamp and something he couldn't decode. "These are very … stylish."

"Ray thought so. Woolies' best – everyone has them. I think they're positively awful, but the whole set was a wedding present from his folks, so I can't complain."

He turned it over. "Homemaker. How apt."

At that moment, they heard the front door slam and a voice call out. "Sorry, love. They didn't have everything at the Royal Oak, so I had to trek all the way to …"

The voice's owner walked in, halting at the sight of strangers in his kitchen. "What the heck? Who are you?"

It took Pol a while to calm him down enough to deliver the newspaper-wrapped package. As she opened it, an acrid combination of vinegar and spices assaulted their nostrils.

Georgie was impressed with Kev's ability to remain impassive, but the stench invoked a raft of memories. Her gran had always blamed the weird cravings on her pregnancies, saying the third was undoubtedly the worst.

Her grandad gestured at the stinking mix of pickled onions, gherkins and eggs. "I keep telling her the bab will come out a right sourpuss with all that vinegar, but she won't have it." He reached in his pocket, retrieving two small bags which he tossed on the table. "And a lard-arse." He guffawed as she pursed her lips.

"Pork scratchings are no' but fat and salt – everything bad for a growing baby. At least that's what the midwife said." He nudged her arm. "But my Pol won't hear a word against it. Reckons it didn't do the first two any harm."

73

"How are the boys?" Kev glanced upwards. "They're very quiet."

"I should hope so. We'd be strung up if we didn't have them in bed by eight-thirty."

Kev's frown asked who by? But he didn't voice it.

"I know what you're thinking. It's the summer holidays, but tomorrow's going to be a long enough day what with the match and all."

"You're taking them to the final?"

A scoff. "Even if they were old enough, we're not made of money. Without the extra from Pol's little job ..." He sucked air through his teeth. "Their uncle's having them for the day – they're dead excited because they get to drive in a posh Jaguar and stay overnight in his country mansion."

"Your brother drives an E-Type?" Kev perked up.

"Don't be daft, how would all their gear fit in one of those?" Ray paused, glass in hand. "Wait – you don't have kids, do you?" He swigged back the ale.

Georgie took Kev's hand, flashing a mournful look. "Not yet."

"Not for the want of trying, I'll bet, eh?" Wiping off the froth with the back of his hand, he chuckled.

"Nudge, nudge, wink, wink as they say in the Latin Quarter." Kev responded automatically.

"What? I don't get it."

"You know. Monty Python." Too late, Kev realised his mistake, trying to cover the panic by gulping his tea.

"Take no notice of him. It's a daft thing his mates do if someone says something even the tiniest bit rude."

He slapped the table. "I like it. "How's it go again?"

"Nudge, nudge, wink, wink." Kev did the actions.

He copied it with gusto. "My mates will love it. Would you like an ale? Or there's Guinness if you prefer. I got it for Pol but she never has more than a couple of sips then turns her nose up."

She shuddered. "They say it's good for you but I'd much rather have a nice cup of tea."

Georgie smiled. "Have you tried it with cheese and biscuits? Or anything salty."

"Pork scratchings?"

"Sure, why not?"

She shrugged. "I'll try anything once."

Ray leapt up. "I can't remember meeting you two before, but you're definitely our kind of people. Even if you do speak a bit funny and have some strange notions about things." He tottered toward the fridge, his gait suggesting he'd downed more than one on his recent hunting expedition.

"That's what happens when we both come from big families." Pol covered Georgie's hand. "I'm sure you'll catch soon, love. He only has to look at me and bang – I'm back up the duff."

He returned with glasses and bottles. "I reckon it runs in the family looking at all our brothers and uncles."

"If you could bottle it, you'd make a fortune." Another foot-shaped-mouth comment from Kev had Ray pausing for an instant.

He shook his head and resumed the pouring. "Sorry, don't get it."

"With two upstairs and another on the way? I think you

do, old chap." Kev winked.

"Ha-ha-ha. You're what my gran would call a card."

"I've been called worse things." Kev accepted the glass and took a sip.

"When's this one due?" Georgie strove to change the subject which was obviously confusing Ray and making Pol uncomfortable. "You look ready to pop."

"Not at all. The midwife reckons at least a fortnight."

"Well the others were late, so you should be fine tomorrow."

"You're going to the match?" Georgie's eyes widened despite her best efforts to control them.

"I've been umming and ahing all week. I really want to support our lads – especially with it being the first time they've made it to the final, and I can't bear the thought of all that money going to waste if I don't go."

"Surely someone would pay full price for the ticket – more even."

"No one I know. All thems as can afford it have bought one, and as for the rest – it's more than a day's pay for most of them. The two tickets we got cost a fortune."

Pol huffed a sigh. "I said it would be better to give the ticket away than waste it, but Ray's convinced it'll all work out for the best."

Georgie caught Kev's eye with a subtle shake of her head as she reached for Pol's hand. "I'm sure his faith won't be misplaced. Let's raise a glass to Bobby and the squad."

As they all clinked their glasses, Ray beamed. "To our lion-hearted lads. My money's on Geoff Hurst to score at least a couple – he's on good form."

Kev's eyes narrowed. "I wonder what odds the bookies would give for that?"

"Three to one. Hardly worth it."

"Wonder what they'd give for a hat trick?" He pointedly ignored Georgie's glare.

A scoff. "You're kidding aren't you? This is international football at its best. No one's ever scored a hat trick in a World Cup before."

"So it would be worth a fiver of anyone's money, then."

"I don't know anyone who could afford to throw away that much on something so unlikely."

"Not even your brother? The one with the Jag and the mansion?"

Pol tutted. "Ray was exaggerating about that. But anyway, he's not the slightest bit interested in sports. He prefers high-falutin' stuff like theatre and opera."

A wail from upstairs had Pol struggling to her feet.

Ray pulled a face "Leave him, bab. He'll settle on his own. You know what the doc said. If you run to the slightest snuffle, they'll never learn."

She reluctantly sat back down, shooting him a dark look. "Have you heard this nonsense? Probably not if you don't have kids. Everyone's quoting this so-called bible about raising children. It's by an American, Doctor Spock. As if he'd know."

Georgie could tell Kev was itching to say something about Star Trek, but she was fairly sure it was too early for them to have heard of it, so she made a bland comment about everything seeming very different in the States.

Another wail had Pol fidgeting, and Ray sighed. "I suppose I'd better do it, you shouldn't really be running up and downstairs in your condition.

As he left, Pol's concern had her twisting her hands. "I should be going really, it's my job. You mustn't think badly of me, it's just I had a bit of a scare with this one–"

Kev jumped in to reassure. "Don't be daft. That bundle looks heavy and you've been carrying it around for months. You must be exhausted all the time, especially with another two to look after. Let him take a turn, it'll do him good."

"Do you really think so? Most men would scorn him for doing a woman's job. Or tease at the very least."

"Thank goodness they're not here, then." Kev winked. "Who knows how other people live?"

She popped a piece of pork crackling in her mouth and sipped the Guinness, nodding her approval.

Georgie suppressed her qualms about the extra work caused by their visit, figuring Pol would appreciate having another woman around the house. And if all went to plan, they would be well compensated. She hadn't told the others much about the legend of her dad's birth, because she'd forgotten a lot of it. Being in the midst brought back some crucial details and she knew what had to be done. The tricky part would be ensuring Kev didn't tip Ray off about how the big win would lead to a lucrative partnership with Isaac's Grampy Eric. *Heck, who was she kidding?* The real tricky part would be dealing with tomorrow's events.

The following day brought with it a multitude of potential potholes to snag their journey with bumps and jolts. Thankfully, her pep-talk with Kev had him winding back his natural ebullience to a level where he engaged brain before speaking.

Meeting her uncles as pre-schoolers raised all manner of odd feelings, but she discovered Kev's hitherto unknown ability to pacify fractious toddlers. The lads displayed an almost instant adulation, and his inner child had no problem keeping them entertained after breakfast until their uncle whisked them away in his posh car.

At the start of the day, Ray had still cherished ideas of Pol accompanying him to the match. As the morning wore on with her showing more signs of discomfort, the potential dangers became obvious to all but him. He hugged her from behind, his arms wrapped around the bump. "It'll be fine; the walk to the stadium will settle him down. It's probably just a bit of wind from those pickles."

She put a brave face on it. "I'm sure you're right."

"I really don't think that's wise." Georgie tried to dial down her concern. "What if she goes into labour?"

"There's plenty of St John's crew who can help her out. She's probably better off there than at home."

"What if her waters break while you're walking there?"

"Unlikely. She's not due for another couple of weeks you know." He folded his arms, but his face wobbled.

"And what about the crowds? Imagine if she ended up getting an elbow in the belly?" She threw a mute appeal at Kev, who stepped in to help.

"It does seem a tad risky. How long's the walk?"

"A couple of miles, just over half an hour normally."

"But this isn't normal. And then to stand for a couple of hours, it's too much."

"But we'll be sitting down—"

Pol's gasp of pain cut him short as he sprang into action, rubbing her back, then making her lie down on the sofa while he massaged her feet. His obvious embarrassment at this level of nurturing had Georgie pulling Kev into the kitchen to help her make the lunch. As she buttered the pasty white bread, he struggled to open a can of corned beef with the can opener.

"Stop. You're supposed to use the key."

"How?"

She showed him the tab, but he put it upside down in the key's slot and wondered why it wouldn't turn.

"Oh for goodness sake, give it here."

"No, I've got it now. The handle should be on the outside. I can't help it if I've never seen one before."

"Just be careful when you bend the tab – if it breaks off it's a nightmare."

"Why do they have to make the tin base rectangular? If it was round you could use a normal opener."

"I have no idea. But be careful, it leaves a really sharp edge that bites back." She grinned. "Gran always kept a can in the cupboard for emergencies. Her corned beef hash was a thing of wonder and only took twenty minutes to make."

When they'd finished, Georgie gazed at the plates, shaking her head. "How did people live like this?"

Kev frowned. "Apart from using brown bread, this is just like a ploughman's."

She shuddered. "Exactly. Bland and insipid – it's all white, yellow and brown. Where's the red and green?"

"They only had seasonal foods until the seventies."

"It's July. They would at least have had lettuce, cucumber and tomatoes."

A noise curtailed the discussion and Ray walked in, exclaiming at the spread. "Gosh, this looks like a party. Pol wondered if you found the pork pie, but you obviously did. And there's some crisps in the pantry. I'll get them."

Kev's face was a picture as he watched the guy searching in the bag to retrieve a twist of blue paper which he opened up and sprinkled over the crisps. As he shook up the contents Georgie mouthed the word, "salt."

Pol waddled into the kitchen and sat at the table.

"And we'll crack open the dandelion and burdock, it'll wash this lot down nicely." Ray fetched the glass bottle with familiar dimples from neck to label.

Georgie set out the glasses, and he poured generous measures of the treacle-coloured liquid while Kev stared at the bottle, his eyes widening.

~*~

They couldn't be serious, surely? Struggling to see the label properly, Kev tried to make sense of the strange yellow shape embedded in the large pink C. It looked like a cross between a comb and a crown, but his mind transplanted an electron microscope picture which had been plastered all over the media for the better part of two years. As Ray put the bottle down, the six-letter word which had sparked his attention became clear: Corona.

"May Bobby and his Lion Hearts win the day."

Kev had no choice but to accept the glass thrust at him, and raise it, echoing the toast. His first tentative sip proved nothing like as bad as he feared. The sweet, cool liquid –

81

truly a distant cousin of coca cola – fizzed on his tongue.

"Not a fan?" Pol grimaced. "I only have it because they reckon it's good for you."

"Like Guinness?" Georgie grinned.

"Exactly. I think you either love it or hate it."

"Like Marmite." Kev winked.

She shuddered. "*No* one likes that. Bovril's so much better." She poured the rest of her drink in Ray's glass. "Is there any ice-cream soda left?"

He'd just taken a mouthful of pork pie, but he dutifully stood and fetched it from the pantry.

"Thanks love." She squeezed his hand and grinned at Kev. "I hope you're taking notes. This is how to treat your pregnant wife." She offered her glass. "Try some."

He sipped. "Haven't had this since I was a nipper."

"Good, eh?" She giggled. "It magically convinces your mouth you've just eaten a dish of vanilla ice cream."

"I would have said best Cornish. Truly scrumptious."

"Good to see you laughing again, Pol. Are you feeling better?" Ray's intent was transparent.

"Better, yes. But not well enough to go to the match. Why don't you go instead, Ken? That is, if you want to. Not everyone's football crazy."

"Are you kidding? It would be the opportunity of a lifetime." He glanced at Ray. "Unless you know someone else."

"I already said not."

"In that case, I'd be thrilled. I'll pay you for the ticket, of course."

"Keep your money, I wouldn't dream of asking. We'd

best be making tracks, the match starts at three and the queues will be lengthy."

Kev knew any attempts to insist would not go down well – Ray was a proud man. They'd worked out a scheme to repay the kindness, and not just by buying the chippy tea he was sure they'd have after the match. He had to credit Georgie with the idea and had every confidence they could pull it off.

Ch 7 – World Cup

30 July 66/Jul 2022

The journey started with a visit to Ladbrokes betting shop where Kev pulled out an impossibly large blue note, putting it on Geoff Hurst to score in the first twenty minutes, handing over the slip. "There you go. Those odds should pay for our food and board for a couple of days."

Ray scoffed "We've gone through this already. I can't take your money."

"It's not mine, it's the bookies."

He put it in his wallet, taking out a crumpled green note. "You think I should put this on Hurst getting a brace?"

Kev squinted at the unfamiliar notes in the dingy light and fished out a red one with the number ten on it. "I'm so sure, I'll double it."

"Are you having me on? How can ten bob ever be double a quid?"

"Sorry. I thought this was a tenner and yours was a fiver." He shuffled in his wallet and brought out the correct note – far more brown than red.

The guy behind had clearly been listening in. "I know what you mean, mate. All the changes in the notes confuse the hell out of me. Mind you, it's not as bad as during the war when they changed all the colours to foil the Nazis."

Despite being far too young to have much to do with war-time money, Kev jumped on the lifeline. "You'd think they'd choose less similar colours."

Staring at the notes, Ray fingered the single fiver in his wallet, muttering something unintelligible. The chap

84

behind the counter read out the odds, his tone bored.

"Just a second." Kev took a gamble on this bit working. "What would it be for a hat trick?"

Raising an eyebrow, the guy looked it up. "It's your money, but I feel honour-bound to remind you no one's ever scored one in a World Cup final."

Shaking his head, Ray worked out the return. "Blimey, Ken. That would be a lifesaver."

"Yep. I reckon those lads must be costing you a pretty penny or two. Think what you could buy for them."

"Bikes for starters. New ones, not second-hand rust-buckets from the rag-and-bone yard." He pursed his lips.

The bookie scowled. "I *do* have other customers."

Ray gulped. "Are you sure? A whole fiver sure?"

"Never been surer." Kev put a hand on his heart. "I feel it in my water. But look, if it's too rich, just do a quid."

With a groan, Ray laid his fiver on the counter.

Kev covered it with the tenner, peering at the guy. "You'll be able to fund that if we drop in on the way back from the match, yes?"

Sniffing, he gestured at the packed shop. "Everyone's gone mad today – football fever at its worst."

"Or best. We're united by a common cause."

"So that's fifteen pounds on Geoff Hurst to score a hat trick at a hundred and eleven to one."

Ray closed his eyes and breathed deeply. Snapping his eyes open, he waved a hand. "Do it."

Kev nodded, waiting for the receipt as Ray lurched toward the door, clamping his mouth. He found him leaning on the wall outside the shop.

"What have I done?" Ray's face wobbled. "Two pounds of that was for the rent and rates, and another was for this month's Christmas club. Pol's going to kill me."

Kev put a hand on his arm. "Don't worry. If the bets don't work, I'll return your fiver."

He shrugged it off. "I'm not a charity case, you know."

"I certainly *do* know. You're an extremely generous man who's taken in a couple of strangers and treated them like royalty. Because you won't accept any money, I'd like to repay you this way. I was gifted this money from someone who tasked me to invest it wisely. Please don't let my good fortune ruin the day. Chin up, mate."

He shook his head. "You're not like anyone I've ever met before. Even aside from the strange notions." He sprang away from the wall. "Come on, if we get a move on there'll be time for a pint."

They covered the majority of the distance at a trot and, when they passed a pub, Ray pulled him in, ordering two pints of Worthington E for the princely sum of five shillings. With an ironic chuckle, Kev selected the ten-bob note and followed his host to stand by a wall whose ledge was barely wide enough for the squat, dimpled pint jug.

Ray knew several people in the pub and a chap in a West Ham scarf sought his opinion over "that dirty scumbag Rattin taking a pop at Charlton and Hurst in the quarter final."

"Thank goodness he didn't nobble either of them."

"Too right. I've put a quid on Hurst, Moore and Peters to score."

"That's daft, Ned." A guy in a Man U scarf mocked.

"Moore's playing at the back. My money's on Bobby Charlton and Roger Hunt – they've three goals apiece."

"True, but Hurst is on great form–"

"Not good enough for Ramsey to pick him for the group matches." The Man U fan cut Ray off, wagging a finger.

He was undeterred. "More's the pity. He scored forty goals last season."

"And let's not forget we wouldn't have made it to the semis without him." Ned gestured his pint at Kev. "Who's your friend? One of your cousins?"

"Close. Married to one of Pol's. This is Ken."

"Who do you support?"

As all eyes turned expectantly, Kev faltered. "Today, it's England. Normally I'm a rugger man."

Wincing at the raft of good-natured abuse, he hoped none of them asked which team. He really needed practice to avoid these foot-shaped-mouth moments.

Thankfully, someone in the bar started a chant and everyone joined in, relieving the pressure.

Ray glanced at his watch. "Sup up. We need to get cracking if we want to get seated before it starts."

The pub was close to the ground and before long Kev spotted the legendary twin towers. They soaked up the atmosphere on Wembley Way, joining in with the good-natured banter as they queued for turnstile D. He couldn't help but contrast with the level of tight-lipped security guards necessary for a modern-day match of this nature. As the crowd of enthusiastic strangers surged around him, he happily tuned into the hive-mind of like-minded individuals intent on cheering their brave lads to victory. Despite everything he knew about how it would play out, Kev felt a thrill of anticipation knotting his insides.

He had a moment's pause, wondering whether Georgie should be here instead of him. But there was only one ticket and the blokey chauvinism in the pub might have spoilt the experience for her millennial sensibilities. More to the point, what use would he be to a woman in labour?

Since realising exactly what her time-travel trip would involve, Georgie had focussed her research efforts in preparation for this moment. She already had rudimentary midwifery knowledge from helping out at her mate's farm during lambing season, and she augmented it with detail gleaned from the internet and several episodes of *Call the Midwife* where she fast-forwarded through to the wet work.

She had the advantage of knowing the baby – *her dad* – would emerge moments after Geoff Hurst scored the final goal, and that her gran had managed without any medical aid. The details of this oft-repeated tale had become less defined over the years, but Georgie knew she hadn't been alone. Strangely, her close relationship with her gran had in many ways prepared her for this. The avid belief in living in harmony with nature and holistic healing methods had set Georgie on her path. So it had all come full circle. Now it was merely hours away, Georgie's natural qualms kicked in and she tried to distract herself with tasks.

Surreptitiously, she'd clocked the whereabouts of essential supplies such as towels, pegs and a Pyrex jug for sterilising the scissors. While clearing away after lunch, she gave the washing-up bowl an extra scrub, assuming she'd be using that to wash the baby. *But what with?* A tea towel seemed obvious, but there were none in the drawer. She regretted asking as soon as the words were out as Pol insisted on climbing the stairs, hanging onto the bannister.

"You didn't need to come, I could have got them. Presumably they're in the airing cupboard."

"That's why I wanted to come. Bless him, Ray's been insisting on putting the washing away for the past few weeks after the midwife said I mustn't raise my arms above my shoulders because it could harm the baby."

Georgie nodded. "I've heard that."

"Anyway, it would be a huge help if you can give me a hand to straighten it all out."

As they worked, Pol told stories of her first two pregnancies, how the eldest lad had continually moved to a position which trapped a nerve and her leg collapsed.

"That must have been scary."

"It certainly was, especially because I didn't have a clue what was happening. And almost as painful as childbirth."

"But not as long, I would guess."

"You'd be surprised. Billy was ready by the time I reached the hospital – they didn't have time to give me a shave, let alone an enema. I was glad because I didn't want all the drugs, and he popped out an hour later."

"That was quick. I've heard it can go on for hours."

"Because they make you lie down. I did all the hard work at home, standing up. And the second took even less time, so the midwife said she'll just get a pail for this one."

Georgie found a stack of nappies which had been shoved to the back.

Pol grinned when she saw them. "I'm glad you found those, I meant to have them handy for when this one comes." She drew in a sharp breath. "Which may be sooner than we think." She glanced at her watch. "We should go down now; the match'll be starting any minute. Just time to boil the kettle."

Georgie went first, switching the TV on so it could warm up then running through to fill the kettle. She was pretty convinced Pol had recognised the "nesting" sign – even if it was sorting rather than the traditional cleaning. All the talk about childbirth suggested she knew on some level – however subliminal.

She'd timed it perfectly and, as she put the tea-tray down on the coffee table, the screen lit up, showing the two teams coming out of the tunnel. The BBC commentator, Kenneth Wolstenholme, eulogised how the Germans had been the world champions twelve years earlier, whereas England had never before got higher than the quarter finals.

"I guess we've missed the pre-match chat about the journey to the final." Georgie cursed herself as she realised they may not have done this in sixty-six, and Pol's curious glance seemed to confirm it.

"You mean how England scored seven goals and only let in one, but the Jerries scored a whopping thirteen?"

"Golly gosh." Georgie remembered one of her gran's catch-phrases for surprise. "I never realised they'd scored nearly double. They must be favourites to win."

"Crikey Mary. Where have you been for the past four days? The news has been full of facts like that."

They focussed as Wolstenholme announced that Bobby

Moore had won the coin toss and elected to kick off. Georgie hadn't realised her gran was so knowledgeable about "the beautiful game," it was a side she'd never seen. She wished she'd paid a bit more attention when Kev was studying it, but she hadn't wanted to risk putting her foot in it by talking about stuff she couldn't possibly have known. After watching so many recent matches on a massive, high quality OLED screen, Georgie had to adjust her mind-set to deal with the amateurish production values, lack of instant statistics and tiny, blurry figures in shades of grey.

Pol was riveted, supping her tea and occasionally rubbing her bump. She clapped the early goal – even though it was the opposition – peering intently at the action replay. Getting up slowly, she gasped and stood behind the sofa, hanging onto it with one hand as she bent over, stretching out her hamstrings.

"Everything okay?"

"A bit of a cramp. I'm sure it's just wind." She squeezed Georgie's shoulder. "I really appreciate you staying with me. Ray's been looking forward to this for so long. Even if …"

She broke off, clutching the sofa, but not before Georgie sensed trouble in paradise. "I'm sure Ken appreciates going to the final. It's the chance of a lifetime."

~*~

Only having been to a couple of top league matches, Kev didn't have much to compare it to. His over-riding impression was of how much more middle-class the sixties match seemed. Men wore shirts, jackets and ties, with only a few sporting flag-infested paraphernalia. No face paints or dyed hair, and not a mask anywhere! In particular, he was struck by the polite, cordial atmosphere – no sign of aggression between rival fans, as though they regarded each other as friendly enemies.

Haller's early goal had subdued the crowd, but Kev felt anticipation grow as Oberath brought Bobby Moore down. He bounced up to take the free kick, and the floating cross found an unmarked Hurst who headed it in as though the play had been practised a hundred times. Which Kev thought it probably had. The resulting equaliser was met with a wall of noise as the stadium erupted with glee. As Hurst jumped up and down on the pitch, Ray clutched Kev's arm. "That's one." He patted his wallet pocket. "And a nice little nest egg."

The rest of the first half saw fairly even possession, with neither side showing any particular sparkle. Every time the ball came within striking distance of a Hammers player, they could hear Ned bellowing, even though he was right at the front. Hurst had another chance with a header on target and the crowd roared. Ray again gripped Kev's arm, but the German goalie punched it away. From that point on, almost every cross or corner lobbed into the box was headed away unchallenged. Kev couldn't help but compare it to modern matches where much more emphasis was placed on precision, pace and finishing. A final corner, taken by Held, saw Banks stop Emmerich's shot, but the ball bounced out to give Oberath a second chance. The German fans were cheering, but Banks managed to curl over the ball this time.

"That was blinking close." Ray huffed a heartfelt sigh.

92

Kev mimed wiping sweat from his brow. "Definitely looking a little ragged."

"It must be half time. Where's the ref?" As he spoke, the whistle blew, and all around people were shaking the hands of strangers with many an eye rolled in relief.

As the players went off, a brass band came on and the light rain turned torrential in its attempt to muddy the pitch.

~*~

When the whistle went for half-time, Pol thanked the Lord and hustled to the outside loo. Georgie wondered if her gran was trying to disguise her labour pains so as not to cause any anxiety on Georgie's part. She'd heard tales of women not even knowing they were in labour until the head crowned, but found it difficult to believe. But unless she'd misremembered, she still had plenty of time, so another cuppa was in order, with maybe a slice of toast and some cheese to give her the energy.

Pol walked into the kitchen, shaking her umbrella and sniffing the air. "Oh my goodness, that's exactly what I fancy, cheese and toast. How on earth did you know?"

She grinned. "A wild guess. It's a while since lunch and I fancied a snack. There's never a wrong time for toast."

"I never thought about it, but you're right." She took a piece, glistening with golden butter and bit off the corner, murmuring appreciation as Georgie took the tray through.

The next half hour could have been the best football ever played and Georgie wouldn't have been able to recall a single move. Ninety percent of her attention tuned itself into her gran's attempts to suffer in silence. Talk about a stiff upper lip! It was a repeat of the first half, with the supping and rubbing, plus additional munching. She stood even earlier this time, claiming that sitting for too long always got uncomfortable.

~*~

At half time, Kev followed Ray up to the concourse, joining in the high spirits, committing every moment to memory to pass on to the others. The excitement of the fans more than made up for the lacklustre pies, and he burst into a spontaneous chorus of "Three lions on a shirt," but the next line about 'Jules Rimet still gleaming' made him realise he couldn't sing the rest and he broke off abruptly.

"What's that? Sounds bizarre. But clever."

"Something I heard, but I don't remember the rest apart from, "Football's coming home, it's coming home."

Ray shot him a quizzical look. "Don't give up your day job, mate. Can't see that bit catching on."

Kev couldn't resist. "Must be the way I tell 'em."

They retook their seats as Germany came out fighting, with Schulz sending Bobby Charlton sprawling in the first thirty seconds, gaining disgusted boos all over the ground. Kev could only admire the way he bounced back and got on with it, even swapping a brief hand-clasp with his opponent. No screaming, holding his head or wasting precious minutes on treatment for a non-existent injury. The resulting penalty appeal was waved away, to accompanying boos from the crowd, but it was clear the German's half-time pep talk suggested a change of tactics leading to three corners in a row.

In England's only shot on target in the second half, Martin Peters beat the German keeper from eight yards to put England ahead. As Peters galloped around the pitch like a prize stallion, Kev joined everyone around him as they jumped to their feet as one, yelling, hugging and happy-dancing as though they were on a Tik-Tok video.

With only twelve minutes to go, no-one felt inclined to sit back down. Most of the home crowd were convinced they'd all but won, however a certain element got greedy, chanting: "we want three!" None shouted louder than Ray – he had so much riding on the hat-trick, but Hurst didn't oblige, spending more time out of the box than in it.

In their efforts to please, the England squad diced with danger twice. Nerves kicked in and the crowd began to whistle for the end. Then, in the eighty-ninth minute, Jack Charlton conceded a free kick taken by Emmerich. Several others helped on the way to Weber, who levelled the score at 2–2, forcing the match into extra time and Ray's face to lighten by several shades at the reprieve.

A despondent silence settled on the home crowd during the break, and Kev noticed a middle-aged man sobbing uncontrollably as his friends tried to console him. He obviously thought it was all over – little did he know!

Ten minutes into extra time, Hurst mustered the energy to catch and control a cross from Ball, sending it up to hit the underside of the crossbar. It bounced down behind Tilkowski and out. Roger Hunt shouted: 'It's there!' and wheeled away as Ray gave the air a victory punch, only to wither as several German players signalled their protests.

In the highest tension of the match, they watched as the Swiss referee consulted with his Soviet linesman. Those spectators who weren't shouting their opinions held their breath, and Kev could imagine families all over England crowded around their tiny TV sets doing the same.

Despite knowing the outcome, he felt the seconds draw out into mammoth epochs until eventually Dienst blew his whistle and gestured, awarding the goal to heartfelt applause. The screaming pierced ears and, as one flag after another threatened to take his eye out, Kev took a moment to savour the fact that he was actually here, at Wembley watching history being made.

With a huge grin, Ray held up two fingers in a victory V, palm outward, reminding Kev of Churchill's salute.

As the minutes ticked down, Ray could barely look, a third goal from Hurst looking less and less likely. Amid the deafening crowd noise, the referee glanced at his watch and put his whistle in his mouth. With seconds to go, Bobby Moore won the ball and, despite Jack Charlton screaming for him to get it out of the ground, he picked out the unmarked Geoff Hurst with a long pass upfield. Kev nudged Ray. "You'll want to watch this."

Hurst thundered forward, ignoring the approaching defender and spectators streaming onto the field, and a superb left-foot smash completed an historic hat-trick to secure victory. The whistle blew to end the match and the crowd went wild. The sea of Union flags jubilantly being waved said it was definitely all over for Germany.

Ray stared as though in shock for several seconds and then blinked. "You've done it. You've blinking-well done it." He pumped Kev's arm up and down. "A blooming hat-trick. Some kind of wizard, you are. Wait till I tell Pol!"

As the Queen, dressed in buttercup yellow with a

matching hat, presented the elegant trophy to Bobby Moore, the colour drained from Ray's face. "Polly."

"What's wrong?"

"She's in trouble." He started moving through the crowd of oblivious strangers, hugging each other and making a lot of noise as the players trotted around the pitch in a lap of honour, some of them dancing in delight.

Kev struggled to catch him up. "What kind of trouble? Is it the baby?"

"I don't know. She's in pain."

It felt a tad far-fetched, but Kev had no doubt Georgie would put it down to a psychic bond formed between them during the pregnancy.

~*~

Pol screamed when Peters scored, quickly assuring it was excitement, not pain. Georgie fancied she could hear echoes from several of the neighbouring houses.

The triumphant celebrations had barely died down when Pol gasped, clutching her belly. "Oh dear. I've a feeling this one doesn't want to wait another fortnight."

Georgie snapped her head around. "You're in labour?"

"Possibly. At first I thought it was merely the practice pains, but there was nothing false about that."

She jumped up. "What do you need me to do?"

"Nothing yet. I wouldn't normally call the midwife until the contractions are less than five minutes apart–"

"What about if your waters break?" This was suddenly getting real. "Should I get some towels just in case?"

"The ones we sorted earlier you mean?" She winked. "That could be useful. And there's a small case in my

97

bedroom with a change of clothes and stuff. They tell you to prepare it a month before in case of emergencies."

Georgie returned as Weber brought the score to two-all, meaning they had to play half an hour extra time. "That's a shame – they could have got it all done and dusted before–"

"Not at all, it's been the best distraction from the pain. Sorry to be a nuisance, but would you mind fetching a couple of pillows from the blanket box?"

"No probs – I mean problem." Running upstairs, she noticed Pol hobbling outside again. She picked up the pile of nappies, and gathered the other bits and pieces before putting the kettle on as Pol returned.

"Oh dear. This chap seems in an awful hurry – my waters just broke."

"Is that normal? How do I get hold of the midwife?"

"Firstly, there's no such thing as normal. Every birth is different. Secondly, there's no chance of calling her – I tried to say earlier. She'll be at the match, and the only other one I like is away for the week."

"Surely there are others–"

"Neither of whom I want in my house. I'd rather it was just us. It feels right. I've done it twice before and it ran smoothly both times. Despite your lack of experience, I have every confidence it'll be equally straightforward."

The absolute faith forged a shiver of encouragement which straightened Georgie's spine and strengthened her resolve. Pol's trust would not be misplaced.

Ch 8 – A Bully's Comeuppance

April 1940

When they arrived back in the attic, mere moments after leaving, Kev dashed straight to the bathroom, barely making it in time.

"Oh dear. He looked a tad green around the gills." Isaac typed on his tablet. "Was it the same on the way there?"

"Not at all. We landed in the rain and he took to it like a duck to water." Georgie grinned.

"But you look a lot better." Ben squeezed her arm. "I guess you're getting used to it."

"Or it could be because they're my dice so I'm in charge. Like you never get car sick when you're driving."

"That's an excellent point." Isaac made another note.

Jen dashed up to hug Georgie. "No side effects at all?"

"Nope. Much easier this time." A wink. "Apart from helping to give birth to my dad. Bet there's not many who can claim to have done that."

"Of course." Jen grinned. "I bet it was wonderful–"

"Spare us the details, please." Isaac shuddered as Kev returned, wiping his mouth.

Jen was undeterred. "–even if was weird holding your own father all greasy with vernix."

"There was loads of it because he was two weeks premature. It was really hard to wash off."

Kev grimaced. "That's way too much information. I can't believe I avoided all the graphic bits over there only to have you spouting gory details here."

Jen chuckled. "Vernix isn't gory; it's the waxy white

stuff protecting the baby's skin."

"I know what it is, thank you very much. I'd just rather not have it discussed in my presence."

Ben raised a brow. "Since when were you squeamish?"

"Yeah, well there's a lot of things you don't know about me, mate. I need a beer." He stalked out.

"Oh dear. Was it something we said?" Isaac pouted.

"I guess he's tired. The time travel takes it out of you. I'll have a word with him." Ben took a step to the door.

Georgie tugged his arm. "I don't think so. He probably just needs a moment or two to adjust. Our bodies think it's eleven o'clock on Sunday morning, and we've not long had a fry-up. Have you guys eaten?"

The trio of shaken heads had her suggesting they did that while she had a quick chat. She found him in the den, sitting on the sofa with a can of Stella and not a single screen switched on. Plonking herself next to him, she nudged his arm. "All right, mate?"

He shook his head as though clearing it, then covered his face with his hands, and she figured her best option was to let him speak when he was ready.

After a few moments, he sat back, swigged from the can and studied her, shaking his head. "Shit, Georgie. What did we just do? How can you be so calm about it all?"

She shrugged. "It is pretty mind-bending, isn't it?"

"You can say that again."

"I could, but I suspect you wouldn't laugh after what you've just been through."

He scoffed. "I know you're strong, but hell. You just delivered a baby. Not any old baby, but your own dad. My

100

brain's going into spasms just trying to work it out."

"Breathe, Kev. Just breathe. When you put it against some of the adventures you've had, it pales into insignificance. I could never–"

Taking her hands, he squeezed them. "Bollocks, Pet. There's nothing you couldn't do. You have more courage than almost every man I've ever met. Same with Jen. The pair of you are like …" He shrugged. "Super heroes."

She smiled, gazing into his eyes. "Bless you for recognising that, but right back atcha."

"No way. I couldn't have done what you did."

"Really? Are you sure about that? I reckon you would have figured out what to do if push came to shove." She chuckled. "Pun not intended, but still funny."

Releasing her hands, he shook his head. "I'm sure you're wrong, but I'm glad you think that about me."

Their faces were close, and if she had a fraction of the gumption he credited her with, she'd have kissed him, but scared little Georgie trembled at the idea of his rejection.

The spell broke as Isaac bounded in. "It's a total long shot, but would you two be up for a quick session?" Oblivious to the moment he'd just shattered, he explained how a short scene now would reduce Saturday's marathon.

Kev shrugged. "Sure, I'm game for a laugh if you are."

"Yeah. Maybe give us ten minutes to get our heads back in the game. It's the audition scene, right?"

"Yes. And it'll be more like half an hour. We wanted to give you time to prepare. Sure you're not hungry?"

"Nope. I'm stuffed." Kev got out his phone.

"Maybe some cheese and biscuits." Georgie followed

Isaac out, reaching the kitchen to be met by anxious faces. "He's fine; a bit jet-lagged and suitably discombobulated. But no more than you'd expect."

"Good." Ben huffed a sigh. "I've never seen him so fazed by anything. How was he over there?"

"Pretty much as you'd expect. Getting it right most of the time with the occasional hiccup."

"Like the rest of us. That's a relief." He backpedalled. "Not that I expected anything else, it's just …"

"I'd throw that shovel away now, mate." Jen winked. "He was a tad wound up after all the shenanigans."

Leaving them to it, Georgie ran up to get her notebook and phone, picking up some nibbles and a couple of slices of garlic bread on her way past the kitchen.

Kev sniffed the air.

"I figured if the others are all gonna be reeking of it …"

"Good call." He swiped a piece and she gave him a tea plate, knowing he'd not resist some cheese, crackers and pickled onion. "That reminds me. I discovered why corned beef cans are rectangular. It was so they could pack them more efficiently for military ops – they take up less space than round ones because they stack better."

"Exactly. And the key meant the squaddies wouldn't starve for lack of a can opener."

"As long as the tab didn't break off." A finger wagged.

She chuckled. He was back on form.

Hettie was a lot happier since Clive arranged for her to take the place in June's billet. The four found themselves meeting regularly, and took to rehearsing scenes from the play together when they shared breaks.

After one of these, Hettie had a parcel for the accounts office, but her entry to the office was blocked by two burly men whose dress and manner reminded her of military policemen, although they weren't in uniform. Between them, head down so his hat obscured his face, was a scrawny character she recognised.

After delivering the package, she passed by a gaggle of women and Lily beckoned her over.

"Was that who I think it was?"

"If you were thinking of Harrington, then yes."

"Good riddance, I say. He was a nasty bully." A petite blonde girl wrinkled her nose.

Amid the murmurs of agreement, Lily's voice lowered. "I think those men were MI5 agents."

"They certainly looked like they meant business, and they refused to tell us anything." The blonde shuddered.

Lily's voice wobbled. "What will happen to him?"

"Nothing he doesn't deserve. I hope they lock him up and throw away the key." Several girls agreed.

"They won't … torture him will they?" Lily paled.

Hettie patted her arm. "He looks like the type who will spill his guts without them even asking."

She looked relieved. "Good. I couldn't bear the thought of … that because of me."

"What did you do?" Hettie stiffened.

"I told Miss M about what you told me – him knocking over your papers so he could read them."

She closed her eyes, guessing at the trouble to come.

"I didn't mention your name; another messenger told

me the same thing. Miss M was far more interested when I asked why such a clever man was doing this kind of job."

"You thought him clever?" Hettie had no evidence.

"Yes. He seemed to know a lot about everything."

"Or he wanted us to believe he did." The blonde added.

"No, he really did. I heard him on the telephone talking about some technical Naval stuff. I only knew because my husband's on that ship." She glanced down. "He never told me, but he talks in his sleep. I never let on I knew."

The supervisor returned from her break, nagging the girls to get back to work. Hettie slid out, not sure what to do about the news and her role in it. But she had a job to do which kept her busy all the way to the evening's auditions.

Birch took his directorial duties seriously, subjecting all the hopefuls to a ten-minute screening in front of a panel which included Ian Fleming and two amateur performers who'd played the leads in several prior productions.

Hettie sat outside the snug, preparing the piece she'd been given to read. He'd asked for a short monologue and the verse or chorus of the song of her choice. Her eyes widened at the tuneful voice coming out from the small room – surely that couldn't be Edward singing *Nature Boy*? She'd never have expected such a soulful rendition from someone so studious. But he'd been called in immediately before her, and no one else had gone in, so it must be him. It had been one of her mum's favourite songs, and it brought a lump to her throat.

On her turn, the great man seemed much more stressed than his normal laid-back, jovial self. "We're running a tad late. Can we go straight to the reading, please?" He gestured at the card in her hand. "Don't worry, we won't expect you to have memorised it."

The added emotion from thinking about her mum helped with the scene, but they gave no reaction, merely scribbling on pads.

Fleming asked her to do the song and, from cold, she went straight into the upbeat version of *In the Mood* with vocals, as done by the Andrews Sisters.

"*Mister Whatchacallim, whatcha doing tonight?*

Hope you're in the mood, because I'm feeling just right ..." She'd studied their delivery, matching their nasal tones and sparky choreography with lots of finger-snapping and shoulder shimmies, but Birch didn't even let her finish the verse before waving her away.

Hettie's face must have shown her disappointment and June looked up in concern as they called her in. She mouthed the words, "All right?" but Hettie gestured for her to hustle – they were not in the mood to be kept waiting.

She joined Edward and Clive, who were celebrating with pints and whiskey chasers.

"Let me buy you a drink." Clive signalled the landlord.

"How did it go?" Ben's cheerful grin nearly undid her. "I'll bet you're a shoo-in for one of the leads."

She shook her head. "I doubt it. They hated me. Didn't want my monologue and I barely sang at all." She nudged his arm. "I heard *your* song though. Who knew you had the voice of an angel hiding under that pipe and deerstalker?"

Clive placed a wineglass in front of her and she sipped, wrinkling her nose. "That's strong. What is it?"

"Port and brandy. Your face said you needed one."

"I didn't know my face could talk. Much less ask for strong liquor. Very clever of it."

"That'll be the actress in you. Every part of your body is a study of eloquence."

Edward slid a glance. "Any excuse to study her body."

Hettie blushed. "Edward Foster, what's got into you?"

His cheeks burnt crimson. "Sorry, did I say that aloud? I have a sneaky inner voice who makes these sarcastic quips, but I don't normally voice them."

Clive raised his glass. "To Eddie's dark horse."

When June appeared, she'd suffered similar treatment at the panel's hands, and Clive had already ordered her a port and brandy in anticipation.

"Thank you, I need this." Her nose twitched in pleasure. "I can see why you looked so down – were they verging on rude to you, too?"

"I felt as though they'd already made up their minds and really couldn't be bothered to waste time seeing me."

"That's exactly how I felt. It came as a shock after Birch's persistent nagging to have a go."

"I guess there are so many more women than men, he's got a wide choice." As Hettie spoke, the red-head strode in, slamming her handbag on the bar.

"Brandy – and make it a large one." She gave them the evil-eye before flouncing back to the landlord, muttering, "too tall. I'll give him too tall."

The four swapped uneasy glances and the men picked up the glasses, retiring to a corner table out of earshot.

"Wouldn't like to get on the wrong side of her." Edward

sipped. "She looks the type who could make trouble."

"Especially if she doesn't get her own way." June leaned forward. "She's got everyone in the decoding room twisted round her little finger – even the supervisor."

Clive snorted. "I know the type. Women want to be her and men want to …" A glance at Edward. "You can guess."

"Not all women." Hettie bridled. "Some of us don't rely on sweet-talking people into doing our bidding."

"Thank goodness." Clive toasted her.

June slid a glance. "You wouldn't refuse. If she said jump, you'd ask how high with your tongue hanging out."

Fleming's appearance curtailed the conversation as he asked Edward and June to accompany him to the snug. They left amid a flurry of nervous glances.

Clive regarded her. "Are you all right? You haven't been yourself all evening."

"I'm not sure it's something I can talk about." She glanced around. "Especially not here."

"Can you give me a clue?" A speculative glance. "It's not that Harrington chap again is it?"

Her eyes widened. "What makes you say that?"

A shrug. "Because he made your life a misery."

"I don't think that will be a problem anymore."

"I see." He scanned the room. "You're right. We can't discuss it here. Can I walk you home later?"

She reached for her glass to cover her uncertainty.

"Strictly business, of course." He glanced around then picked up his pint. "I can't bear waiting."

He'd no sooner taken a sip than Fleming appeared asking them to bring their drinks and follow him.

Hettie clocked the outrage on the red-head's face as they passed the bar, and struggled to comprehend when Birch asked them to run through a scene with her and Clive playing Hero and Claudio.

He gestured at the others. "I believe you know June and Edward, who will be playing Beatrice and Benedick."

"Of course." Clive managed a casual nod.

"I'll read any other parts. Take five to read the scene."

Sending grateful thanks for the chance to gather her wits, Hettie spotted a water jug on a side table and poured a glass, sipping so as not to choke. The next few minutes were a blur as she ignored her body's instinct to collapse, but Clive's smile reassured and she responded gratefully.

At the end, Birch thanked them for their cooperation and waved them out while the "jury conferred."

When they returned to the bar it seemed the other hopefuls had made up their minds it was a done deal as people clapped them on the back and raised glasses. Apart from the red-head's sour puss, everyone in the room smiled with genuine encouragement.

Birch's entrance, flanked by his team prompted a spontaneous round of applause, which he revelled in briefly before signalling a halt, slicing his hands horizontally. "Thank you for all your efforts. We are overwhelmed by the amount of sheer talent in this room."

He read the successful names out in reverse order to their billing, "leaving the best till last." His wink brought a few chuckles; this time-honoured tradition kept people hopeful to the end. As he read out "Rhonda" for the actress playing Ursula, the red-head gasped, flouncing out as another girl muttered, "At least you're not playing a man."

Hettie didn't hear a thing after her name, but the expressions on her three friends' faces suggested they'd landed the other lead parts, and the smiles and generous round of applause said no one other than Rhonda begrudged. The rest of the evening passed in a blur, and she smiled gratefully when Clive offered to walk her home.

Despite their instant and uninvited notoriety, they managed to slide off unnoticed, principally due to his clever wheeze. Following his suggestion, she'd picked up her handbag to "powder her nose," and he met her in the corridor, sneaking out via the side door.

When they'd put a few dozen yards between them and the open windows, she blew a grateful puff of air. "I feel badly about abandoning June."

"Don't worry. Edward will escort her home like the true gentleman he is." He scanned the street and led her past the row of cottages and down the lane to a gap in the hedge.

She folded her arms. "I'm not that sort of girl."

"The sort who needs the seclusion of a field with reasonable visibility before discussing dangerous secrets?"

As though to encourage, the waning moon hid behind the clouds long enough to let them squeeze through the hedge unseen before lighting up their path to a log.

He spread his jacket for her to sit on, then took his place close enough so she didn't have to raise her voice, but leaving a decent gap. "Tell me the latest on Harrington."

"How do I know you won't go straight back to Denniston and turn me in for careless talk?"

"You don't. But I swear on my honour I'm no snitch."

She folded her arms. "You'll have to do better than that. I remember how easily you got me to talk about him earlier. How do I know you're not a spy?"

"You don't." He reached for his cigarettes, offering one and asking if she minded if he smoked. Her head-shake had him lighting it and drawing deeply, obviously a ploy to give him thinking time. He exhaled, taking care not to breathe the smoke at her. "Actually, I lied."

"What?" She stiffened.

A shrug. "It's not what you think. I need you to trust me a little longer till I can explain. Will you do that?" At her less-than-enthusiastic nod, he continued. "So, fire away."

"Remember my friend who told me about him bullying the other messengers?" A nod. "She told Miss M about it without naming names."

"Smart cookie."

"And she mentioned how he seemed too clever for the job he does. I assume that's how they caught him."

"In accounts, right?" When she glanced away, he didn't press. "Is that it?"

"Isn't it enough?" She gulped. "The upshot was two plain-clothes MPs escorting him away this morning."

"How do you know they were MPs?"

A shrug. "The way they acted. Certainly military, if not police – they had that humourless indomitability. I suppose they could have been MI5 – or is it 6?"

Another thinking-time drag. Another considerate exhale. "If I tell you something, will you promise not to repeat it to anyone?" His hard stare made the quip about his lies die on her lips.

"Cross my heart." Her finger echoed the oath.

He chuckled. "You don't need the 'hope to die' bit."

"I wouldn't anyway. It's the last thing I hope for."

"You're right about your friend's information leading to his pulling in for questioning."

"I knew it."

"But of course you cannot tell her how you know that for sure, so you should just emphasise to all your friends that they have a duty to report all suspicious behaviour."

"You mean tell them all to spy on each other? I wouldn't feel right about supporting that." A shudder. "Surely there are enough posters around the place."

He finished his cigarette and ground out the stub. "Of course. But your friend did the right thing in going to Miss M – she's definitely a person who can be trusted."

Hettie relaxed. "We all know that. She pretends to be stern, but she always has a twinkle in her eye."

"Talking of twinkling eyes, you didn't seem overjoyed by the prospect of playing Hero – did you not want the part? I assumed after all your effort …"

She sighed. "No, I'm excited, really. It's just … maybe I'm a little overwhelmed. It's been a long day."

"I'm sorry, here's me keeping you up."

"With good reason." Although later, when sleep eluded, Hettie replayed the conversation and wondered at his motivation – he'd not given anything away. And his face had definitely wobbled when he'd mentioned the reason for Harrington's capture. A lie if ever she heard one.

~*~

Pleased when Isaac suggested calling it a night after her

scene, Georgie figured a hot soak might revive her, but the lavender-scented steam had the opposite effect, so she gave into the idea of a mug of chocolate and an early night.

Jen made the drinks, adding marshmallows, and they sat on the sofa, legs curled up, nibbling luxury cookies.

"I'll understand if you don't want to talk about it right now, but I'm fascinated by the idea of being a birth partner. Was it as bad as you imagined?"

She sipped, wiping the froth moustache. "Not at all."

"I just meant if you're not too tired right now."

"I can't see me sharing it with anyone else – the boys are far too squeamish if Kev's reaction is anything to go by. And there's the whole thing about the memories fading – at least if I tell you, there's a chance you might remember." She pulled out her phone, setting it to record and began with the necessary planning, quickly moving on to Pol's attempts to disguise her labour pains.

Jen pursed her lips. "I've always wondered how I'd react – I like to think I'd cope as bravely as Pol."

"Me too. You hear so many stories. I think the match was a good distraction, she was quite invested."

"So what's the deal with all the towels and boiling water you see in period movies?"

Georgie explained about sterilising everything and how Pol's waters had broken while she went for a pee.

"That was lucky. I think that would be my biggest fear – that it soaked the bed or happened in the car."

"I suspect you're not alone." As she described the wonder of the moment the baby's head emerged, tears filled her eyes. She hadn't appreciated it at the time, but the

112

bond she'd made with her gran after sharing such an intimate act went deeper than any she'd ever experienced.

Something struck her. She and her gran had been extremely close when she moved in with her, and they both had deeply spiritual connections. *So how come Pol never twigged she was the Joy who helped her give birth?*

Ch 9 – Dynamo

May-July 1940

Kev struggled to focus on the game – something Ben didn't need telling as he scooped another stack of free points. "Sorry mate. My head really isn't in it."

"No shit, Sherlock. You may as well just hand me the rest now." He quit the game and raided the cooler for a couple of beers, handing one over as he sat on the sofa, puzzled when Kev just stared at his without opening it. "Are you okay, mate? That's grounds for a trip to A&E."

He shook his head. "Sorry, what?"

Ben gestured at the can. "An intact ring-pull five seconds after it reached your sticky little mitts."

With a blink, he did the necessary and the can's hiss had more than a smidge of relief. After a girl-sized sip he put it on the table and dug the heels of his hands into his eye sockets, grinding as though to rid them of demons.

"Whoa, Kev. You'll crush them to a pulp."

He stopped kneading and cupped his face, scrunching his shoulders. "This is so wrong. What we're doing. I love a time-travel movie as much as the next guy, but we've been meddling in stuff we can't hope to understand."

"We've gotten away with it so far. More by luck than judgement, admittedly, but–"

"How can you be so flip?" Shaking his head he swigged a mouthful, trying to order his thoughts. "What if my meddling with Ray's bets led to some kind of *Back to the Future* paradox?"

With a frown, Ben sat back, crossing a foot over his

114

knee. "What's brought this on? When we mentioned about Georgie and I ending up in a different reality, you were cracking jokes."

"No disrespect, but at that point I thought you guys were all on a wind up. I never believed it for a moment."

"But now you know it's possible …"

"It's a blinking massive responsibility. I'm not sure I'm ready for it." A beat. "Being such a klutz an' all."

"But at least you knew what was gonna happen. Poor Jen had no clue and she was on her own. Georgie was with you, and she'd done it before."

"Yeah, we had no problem with the journeys, and I made a few stupid cock-ups which she smoothed over. But when I was on my own …"

"What did you do?" Ben's tone anticipated disaster.

"Nothing too drastic. Apart from putting an extra bet on in a different bookies."

"Plank. What were you thinking?"

"I did the maths and what Georgie suggested wasn't anything like enough for Ray to ditch his job and go into business with Eric."

"So …"

"So I nipped out in the morning and did an accumulator in Ray's name and put the receipt on the sideboard."

"I bloody knew it."

"What?"

"Isaac said something about not trusting you not to interfere in the past, but I promised him you wouldn't."

"More fool you. If there's one thing you can rely on, it's that I'm unreliable. Except about cocking things up."

"Prat. It's nothing to be proud of, you know."

"Don't preach. If you knew me at all you'd know I'm not proud – I just can't help it. And before you give me the think-before-you-act speech, I get it. And the one about the road to hell being paved with good intentions."

"I was only joking. You get stuff right way more often these days, and let's face it – you got back here so it can't have been all bad."

"Really?" He brightened.

"Yeah. So he probably didn't cash it. It's all good."

The following day saw Georgie up early to sort out an extremely irate garden centre manager. It was all hands on deck to get the beds planted in the morning, as they couldn't do it during the heat of the day. The rest of them decided to carry on – having the party split up happened often in this scenario. After a tasty fry-up, they headed to the games room.

Isaac began with an announcement. "As you might have noticed, there's a war on. That's going to be an important part of this scenario, so you'd better achieve your goals before it finishes. I'm going to move the clock on now."

~>#<~

Denniston addressed the assembled group. "We've had a bit of a setback. It looks as though Jerry has changed the procedure yet again. For everything except yellow traffic they're using new message keys. As a result, the Jeffreys sheets aren't producing anything recognisable, so it's all hands on deck until we can crack the new system."

"What, you mean us girls will be decrypting?" June

assumed that was why they were included in the briefing.

"Some of you, yes. At the moment there are approximately a thousand messages coming in every day."

"No doubt due to the invasion of France, Belgium and the rest." Edward puffed on his pipe.

"Quite. Exactly as when they invaded Norway and Denmark. But what is most concerning is whether their sudden elimination of the repeated message key is because they've discovered we're breaking the codes."

A mix of gasps and gloomy head-shakes greeted this.

"It could be simply that someone figured out what a gift it is to the decryption process." Clive offered.

"So are we back to searching for cribs using rods to check for clicks?" Edward groaned. "I'm guessing *Keine besonderen Ereignisse* isn't going to feature much."

"It's unlikely they'll have 'no special occurrences' to report, so we're back to Turing's idea the word 'eins' appears in ninety percent of messages." Clive sighed.

"That's German for one." June frowned. "And, of course there are no numbers on the machine so they have to spell them all out."

Denniston peered at her. "Who told you that?"

"I worked it out for myself."

"I see. Anyway, the idea is we shall need round-the-clock coverage in order to deal with the huge numbers of messages, and having all available eyes on the problem, we stand a better chance of cracking it. For those of you unfamiliar with decryption techniques, John Herivel will explain his method."

In essence, it relied on the fact the men using the

machines were only human and many of them were lazy. "Why move the wheel twelve notches when two or three are just as random?" He nodded at June's raised hand.

She stuttered in her excitement. "If we c-compared the indicator settings we'd find similar letters being used."

"Precisely. It takes a few before the pattern emerges, but I've seen it done in thirty messages. And the best hit rate is in the ones after the new key is done at midnight."

"Because they'll likely be tired and less accurate."

With a nod, he explained how he'd devised a grid to make the spotting of these "clusters" easier, thus reducing the possibilities down from seventeen thousand to six.

"Should speed things up considerably." Clive grunted.

"Now if you get any three-part messages, the rules say they must all have different indicator settings, and again there are obvious patterns. For example, if the first two are QWE and ASD what is the third?"

After a moment, Edward suggested "ZXC," while June said, "PYX." Clive just frowned.

Without hinting, he tried another set. "QAP and EDX."

"TGV." June took a beat longer while the other two looked puzzled.

"Last one. And I'll give you a clue. Look at the Enigma keyboard. MKO and NJI."

Q W E R T Z U I O

A S D F G H J K

P Y X C V B N M L

June wrote her answer down to give the other two a chance as they stared at the slightly different arrangement:

They answered simultaneously. "BHU."

"You've got it. And these patterns are common in the message keys too. One operator uses opposing pairs, for example LKO for the indicator setting and PAQ for the message key."

"I heard one operator used his girlfriend's name CIL every time."

"That's why we call them Cillies. Repeated letters such as AAA or LLL are common, as are German swear words."

The blackout lasted for five long, tiring days until the combination of Cillies, Herivel tips and the growing expertise brought a breakthrough. Welchman was so impressed with June's quick brain he put her on the midnight till eight shift along with Edward and Clive where her speed and accuracy in completing the Herivel grids produced clusters faster than any other team. They then split up the messages between them to do the subsequent stages. Certain the key lay in the three-part messages, she always nabbed any of these in her pile.

The sheer quantity of messages produced by the blitzkreig made operators even sloppier than normal. Her brain became so attuned to the patterns, she started each session by numbering the messages in her pile and then sorting them so it took less and less time for the clusters of settings to stand out on Herivel square. Obsessed with proving a woman was just as capable as a man, June took to staying on long past her shift and on a couple of days, didn't go home, snatching a few hours' kip in a quiet corner before returning at midnight.

Both Edward and Clive worried about her, taking it upon themselves to ensure she got enough to eat and keeping her supplied with water and tea. Their attempts to coax her outside met with little success and this unhealthy existence took its toll on her appearance with lank hair, waxy complexion and dark circles under her eyes. Finally, on the sixth day, the break came and they were back in. She staggered home and slept for thirty hours without surfacing.

On her return, she was treated very differently by several of the boffins who'd previously bandied around the "silly deb" tag she found so insulting. Now, they sought her opinion and she happily shared her expertise to improve their technique.

A few days later, they huddled round the wireless as news came through that German forces had trapped the Allied forces, including French, Belgian, and British Expeditionary Force along the northern coast of France. The BEF commander General Viscount Gort, had no choice but to re-group to make a stand, picking Dunkirk, the closest decent port. Those who fancied they knew about military strategy suggested the wisdom of this should they have to resort to evacuation across the Channel. The press presented it as a last stand as "our brave lads" pulled back in large numbers to prepare for the siege of Dunkirk.

At the midnight shift change, Denniston gathered everyone together, stressing the importance of decoding every piece of information in the light of some strange intelligence. It appeared one of the generals had issued a halt order which had been approved by Hitler. Although they couldn't fathom the reason, it gave the trapped Allies a bit of breathing space to construct defensive works. "However it seems the message did not include the Luftwaffe who are still attacking. We are prioritising any messages from German High Command, and Welchman has a list of suitable crib words we'd like you to use. Good luck chaps." A beat. "And chapesses."

June swapped eye-rolls with the other women in the room and collected a copy of the cribs which included von Rundstedt, the general who'd requested the halt order.

As luck would have it, the new settings proved one of the toughest yet and, after five hours of trying every technique at their disposal, the team were none the wiser on the day's key. June rubbed her eyes at the rattle of ladders outside as the blackout shutters were removed, letting the pale dawn sun seep in.

In a last-ditch attempt, she spread the six Herivel sheets on her desk and gazed at them, de-focussing her eyes so the letters blurred leaving a vague overall impression.

Something tugged at her mind and she tried stacking three so the grids lined up exactly, holding them over the bulb to reveal the group hiding in plain sight.

Welchman came to her in great excitement. "I think I might have a solution, but I need someone fast on the machine to test my theory."

"Would it have anything to do with the four corners by any chance?" She showed him her sheet.

"Absolutely. I think we should call that a draw."

With the first two letters both being A, Y or Z, they worked out the third letter was most likely E, F or G.

"I'm concerned about the scattering of Ps and Rs." As June pointed to them, Edward turned up with a tray of tea mugs. "Do you know Morse?"

"I have a list here somewhere." She pulled it out. "Oh, I see. The R is dot-dash-dot, but F is dot-dot-dash-dot. They could have missed the first dot if they were in a hurry."

"And G is one less dot than P."

Clive appeared, swiping a mug with thanks. "What's this huddle in aid of? Have you got a breakthrough?"

Welchman explained the far flung cluster. "I can't believe it's never come up before."

"Need any help?" Edward's question had him shaking his head, but June reasoned they had a much better chance if all four of them worked on the cribs to get the correct ring setting and wheel order. Setting up each menu to test took a while and she devised a system to ensure none of them were reinventing wheels. Finally, a short while before the next shift came in, Welchman cracked it.

Everyone stayed on, keen to deal with the flood of messages and it proved to be absolutely vital. The brief pause had allowed the Germans to move significant numbers of troops from all over the region, converging on Dunkirk. The mass of combat intelligence gave an early warning that the military situation was hopeless, and they wasted no time in relaying this information to London.

When the halt order was rescinded on 26 May, the bones of "Operation Dynamo" were already in place. As a result of the Ultra intel from Bletchley, senior commanders were already assembling a fleet of over 800 vessels – including British, French and Canadian Navy destroyers –

when Lord Gort finally announced the decision to evacuate.

A big cheer went up in the hut with the news of the first evacuations, even though only seven thousand Allied soldiers escaped on the first day. News reports celebrated the "Little Ships of Dunkirk," a flotilla of hundreds of merchant marine boats, fishing boats, pleasure craft, yachts, and lifeboats called into service from Britain.

Georgie returned as they took a short break, and when Isaac described the next scene, she was keen to be included for such a historic event. The spymaster set the scene:

The next few days saw a tense mix of fortunes as the Belgian army surrendered, but the French First Army managed to delay seven German divisions for four days at Lille, saving thousands of Allied lives. Everyone at Bletchley huddled around the radio on the fourth of June to hear the Prime Minister address a worried nation.

They had to pay attention to the crackly broadcast as Churchill described the events leading up to a "miracle of deliverance, achieved by valour, perseverance and perfect discipline." After giving due credit to the air force for their part in the rescue operation, he announced the intention that the British Empire and the French Republic will defend to the death their native soil.

The call to arms, intended to rouse spirits, was delivered in the tone of benevolent grandfather, much older than his reported sixty-six years. "Whatever the cost may be, we shall fight on the beaches, in the fields and in the streets." One by one, the people stood, saluting the words as

Churchill vowed "we shall never surrender, but carry on the struggle until the new world steps forward to liberate the old."

"Well if that's not a clear message to the Yanks to help us out, I don't know what is." Clive remarked.

"True. But as he said, wars are not won by evacuations, and this was in no way a victory." Edward added.

Clive scoffed. "The sheer quantity of abandoned equipment made it anything but a success."

"Not forgetting the massive loss of lives." June glared.

Denniston cut her off with a wave of his hand. "I can categorically state our efforts have made a difference, allowing many more lives to be saved. In recognition, I'd like to invite everyone for a drink. I believe the Drunken Arms is a suitable hostelry for such a celebration."

"I believe you mean the Duncombe Arms, sir." Hettie giggled.

He smiled at her. "I have it on good authority I got it right the first time."

~*~

With just over an hour until the final kicked off, they needed something to eat. The breakfast, substantial though it was, wouldn't sustain them through till 6:45.

"Could be even longer if they do extra time." Kev rummaged in the freezer.

"There's confidence." Georgie joshed.

"What are you looking for?" Jen frowned. "I was only thinking a light bite, not a full blown Sunday dinner."

"Something like these?" He produced a box of pizza-style snacks. "They only take fifteen minutes. Or there's

124

some Kentucky-fried chicken wings."

"Do them all. I'm hungry now, and if we're still peckish at the end we can always order in."

During the first half, Kev watched Georgie surreptitiously, feeling a total fraud. She was ten times more passionate about football than he would ever want to be, and by rights, she should have had the experience of watching the cup final with her granddad.

He couldn't help but contrast the playing styles and realised that if he had a couple of grand to bet on the '66 men's team playing the Lionesses, he wouldn't have put it on the men. *Sacrilege!*

After a goalless first half, Ben gestured at the screen. "Bit of a difference to the last match you watched, huh?"

Kev scoffed. "Are you reading my thoughts? I reckon Ramsey's team would have struggled against them. They're way more fierce."

Jen grinned. "Lionesses usually are."

An eye roll. "Because they not only do all the cooking, cleaning, shopping and look after the kids, they do all the hunting while the males lounge around primping their manes."

She chuckled. "Actually I read something recently which says they do get off their arses occasionally, but when they kill, they don't share their food."

"As anyone will know if they ever tried to take a chip off Kev's plate." Georgie slid a glance.

"What is it with you girls? If you want a portion of chips, I'll happily buy you one. But apparently it doesn't taste the same unless you've nicked it off a guy's plate."

Isaac rolled his eyes. "I can't believe you haven't sussed this is all part of the mating ritual. They never steal chips from *my* plate."

They were saved the need to answer by the start of the second half, where Ella Toone's fresh legs after replacing Ellen White saw her scoring the first goal. Even before the happy dancing finished, Lina Magull had a near miss. When she scored a few moments later, they all agreed she deserved the equaliser, even if it did result in extra time.

"Interesting that this echoes the nineteen sixty six final, in that it too was a draw at half time and full time." Isaac had a bunch of theories why the home side should win, but they were all more interested in replenishing their glasses.

When Chloe Kelly scored with only eleven minutes to go, he tried in vain to interest anyone in the fact she too had been a substitute. The final ten minutes, a masterclass of time-wasting tactics, saw Euro victory for England, beating Germany 2–1. The celebrations lasted long into the night.

Ch 10 – Cracking the Code

August 2022

Monday had anti-climax written all over it after the double whammy of defeating the Germans – twice – at football and foiling their wartime attempt to devastate the BEF. Isaac called an extra-ordinary general meeting after dinner to "throw a few ideas about."

"Before you get started, can I throw something else into the mix?" Kev plonked a flash drive on the table.

"What's this?" Isaac's sharp tone said he had an idea.

"All the files on Eric's computer. I figured there might be something in there with a clue to the keys."

"And is there?"

"Not that I've found so far. I figured we'd get there quicker by activating the hive brain."

"Oh, no. You don't have to assimilate us all do you?" Georgie held up her index fingers in a cross.

He chuckled. "Can you imagine how much time that would save us? I've run a few file searches for keywords like password, key and clue, but so far nothing's bitten."

"Because he's obviously going to hide stuff in a file called that." Georgie rolled her eyes.

Kev reeled at her tone. "Not just the file names, but the contents, obviously."

A huff. "Pardon me for not being a tech wizard."

Wondering what provoked this vehemence, he held back, keeping it neutral. "I've included names of the coding techniques, like Enigma, Caesar and Vigenère. If anyone has more ideas, let me know and I'll add them."

Jen got out a notepad, and every time someone thought of a crib, she added it to the list as the five of them tossed around a few ideas of how to tackle the search. In the end, it was Georgie who came up with the best solution after spending some time searching through the directories while she was supposed to be doing the inventory.

When Isaac brought the subject back to the D&D campaign, Ben scanned the room. "I don't know about anyone else, but I'd be happy to put it on hold for a wee while. If there's any chance of us *actually* travelling through time rather than a simulation …" A shrug.

"You said it, mate. Despite the side-effects, I want to go again. I'm in." Kev put his hand in the centre and both girls added theirs, followed by Ben.

Isaac's pursed lips suggested he wasn't happy to be steamrollered into it. "But what about the dangers? You saw the state I got into—"

"Because you used and abused, mate. We've only done it once – apart from Georgie, and she's fine. Come on – put your paw in."

The instant Isaac tentatively reached out toward the stack of joined hands, Kev shouted, "deal." He lifted his hand up to split them apart, making the girls giggle.

Ben sobered, frowning at Isaac. "Before we get too carried away, I need to know how come Kev's presence in 1966 didn't change things. How confident are you this present is the same as the one if he hadn't travelled?"

"You can never be a hundred percent sure, you know, with the potential for multiverses and all that."

"One alternate universe is enough." Georgie shuddered.

"What about the prime directive? You said the rule is you can't change the past." Kev frowned.

"And we didn't." Georgie shrugged. "As I said, one of Gran's cousins turned up the night before with his wife – it must have been us."

"It was the same for me." Jen shook her head. "Somehow, Gran had met a person I always thought was called Jan, but it was me from the future."

"So what about the bets I persuaded Ray to put on? That must have been life-changing, surely?" Kev's face wobbled as Ben glanced up.

Isaac dismissed it. "I can only imagine your actions – or rather *Kenneth's* actions – were necessary for Ray and Eric to go into business and end up owning this place."

"Mind actually blown." Kev mimed a gun to his temple.

Jen's eyes narrowed. "So how can we possibly tell which actions will change the past and which ones won't? I'm thinking of Stepford-Jen and the chavs."

Kev quipped. "Sounds like a grunge band."

"Can't change the past." Isaac smirked.

"Cause an alternate reality, then. Pedant."

Isaac's expression dimmed. "You can't. Tell, I mean."

Georgie frowned. "You're deliberately oversimplifying. Before we go anywhere, we need to research the hell out of it to minimise the impact." She glared at him. "That's how come you know about Ray and Eric."

He glared back. "You really did dig deep into those files, didn't you?"

"What's the point of us honing our research skills if we don't use them? It's something we do well."

Kev stared. "If we restrict jaunts to well-documented events, we can be like benign observers. Wasn't there a Star Trek episode like that?"

"Not to rain on your parade or anything, but at the moment, we're rather limited by only being able to travel to the same date in a year ending in double digits."

"That gives us enough scope for now." Despite the adverse physical effects, Kev's appetite was well and truly whetted, and he had every confidence they'd soon be able to extend beyond these restrictions.

Isaac's face wobbled as he glanced away, alerting to yet another economy with the truth, but no one else noticed. Unwilling to risk a complete loss of cooperation by challenging, Kev figured he'd take the little win now and save the bigger battles for later when he knew more.

"No time like the present." Jen grinned. With her usual efficiency, she'd photocopied the pages Isaac hadn't sussed and distributed them evenly.

Leafing through, Kev spotted a block of numbers:
<u>9</u> 16 7 0 14 20 7 23 0 18 9 16 0 12 16 0 25 11 20 12 0
8 25 3 0 5 0 22 24 14 8 15 3 9 6 9 0 12 3 4 16 0 13 24
0 9 16 7 0 26 12 13 10 20 12 0 17 7 25 9 10 0 21 23 5
5 4 23 23 8 0 23 16 0 4 19 5 12 0 19 9 22 15 , 0 4 5 17
24 22 9 0 19 5 0 5 4 4 3 6 0 4 19 22 23 20 0 2 11 23
16 23 0 20 20 14 17 2 16 0 22 7 1 20 11 24 18 0 24 26
20 0 12 11 13 16 .

A quick check revealed they were all in the range of one to twenty-six, and a key showed the underlined numbers were capitals. He started converting each one to its corresponding letter: IpgOntgwOripOlpO...

It soon became obvious the zeroes were spaces, but it was still time consuming,

"Got something?" Georgie peered over his shoulder.

"Yeah but it'll take all night."

"Looks like an alpha-numeric substitution. You know there's an app for that, right?" She skipped away as he face-palmed, growling, "Of course there is."

A short while later, he got to the end and stared at it.

Ipg ntgw rip lp yktl hyc e vxnhocifi lcdp mx ipg zlmjtl qgyij uweedwwh wp dsel sivo, deqxvi se eddcf dsvwt bkwpw ttnqbp vgatkxr xzt lkmp.

Next step was to try the Vigenère app, so he pulled it up, pasted in the text and ran the auto solve option. The first ten attempts didn't have a single recognisable word.

"Whoop de do." He chucked his phone on the table.

"Something vexes thee?" Jen glanced up.

"Nothing but gibberish." He showed her the screen.

"What max key length are you using?"

"No idea. I thought it was fixed."

She scrolled down and pointed to the auto solve options. "Six is very short. Try a bigger number."

"Right-o. But tomorrow. I've had enough. Night all."

Georgie found him swallowing ibuprofen. "Are you okay, Kev? It's not like you to take pills for anything."

"More of a precaution. I've had this kind of headache before and if I don't get a decent night's kip, it'll turn into a full-blown migraine. You've had no side-effects?"

"Apart from dreaming about those crazy eggs and

gherkins last night."

He grinned. "Well, let's hope I don't dream of pickles."
But that was exactly what happened, although he had no
clue at the time. His dream started off with scenes from an
old black-and-white spy movie he'd watched recently with
Isaac. The scenes changed to a typical sixties *Carry-on*
style film, in full colour. Again about spying, but this one
featured a black and white dog.

In the way dreams do, it hopped between snatches of
other black-and-white movies, with scenes of a heist like
the great train robbery, a museum and a fish-and-chip shop
where everyone wore flat caps like a scene from *Peaky
Blinders*. Like a running gag, the dog appeared in every
scene like some mad "Where's Wally" cameo, but as soon
as Kev spotted him, the scene moved to the next one.

At some point, he fell into a deep sleep, but just before
his alarm went off, the movie-spool re-ran so he awoke
with images of the ubiquitous mutt whose name eluded
him. He fell back to sleep, and when he woke again, he'd
overslept and the others had left without him. Skipping
breakfast, he made it in just before nine and a busy
morning kept him occupied till lunch.

Waiting for the others, he pulled up the app and
changed the max length to 20. The result had actual words,
using the key `pickltjzbbkles`. He couldn't hide his
excitement as they plonked their trays on the table. "OMG.
We're getting closer. But I think it's got another level of
encryption."

"Let me see." Jen studied it. "Why would he put random
garbage in the middle of the word pickles?"

"That's it. Georgie was on about pickled eggs after dreaming about them." He tried it and got even closer:

The dict can be uhed for a sifferect date iu the paiged owneg focussts on thai date, saning it aaoud thrte times qefore rdlling twe dice.

"That sounds like a real breakthrough." Ben beamed. "If we can work out what 'iu the paiged owneg focussts' means. Along with 'saning it aaoud thrte times' – could that be saying it aloud thirty times?"

Isaac scoffed. "Really? Thirty times? How would you keep count? So much for dreams."

"Hold on a second. I dreamt of a dog last night. Its name was Pickles." He chuckled. "After Georgie said she hoped I wouldn't dream of pickles." He deleted the eggs. "Bingo!"

The dice can be used for a different date if the paired owner focusses on that date, saying it aloud three times before rolling the dice.

He had to read it three times before the full implications sunk in and he beamed at her. "So we can go somewhere other than today's date? That opens so many possibilities."

Ben clapped him on the back. "Whoa, mate. Before you get carried away, we should consider Isaac's warning."

"And only go somewhere we can research the hell out of?" He echoed Georgie's phrase with a grin. "I have just the episode in mind."

Ch 11 – A Cup and a Dog

March 1966

Travelling on the tube in London five decades ago had few differences to any recent journeys – it seemed every bit as busy on a Saturday morning as it would be in 2022. The main difference, apart from the obvious fashion/style was the total lack of a mobile phone. Instead, people read books, magazines and huge newspapers – anything rather than engage with the strangers around them. Further up the carriage a couple of families with young kids were obviously sight-seeing. The youngsters must have been drilled with the "children should be seen and not heard" mantra as they sat quietly with no need of gadgets, food or drink to pacify them.

"Joy" and "Ken" swapped meaningful glances as they pulled into their station, joining the orderly queue to exit the train and ascend the escalators to arrive in the heart of Westminster.

"Is it me, or is it all a bit Stepford?" He whispered as they emerged to the sight of Big Ben, unfettered by the scaffolding.

"As in populated by cyborgs?"

"Technically speaking they were androids – no human parts. Sorry, I'll just take my Isaac hat off." He lifted the fedora, and a couple of women walking past said good morning, then dissolved into giggles as they realised neither of them knew him.

"You'd better be careful, looking as good as you do. I think that means you're engaged now."

He replaced the hat, then tucked her arm through his elbow. "That's why I brought a bodyguard. Look fierce and scare them off."

"And here was me thinking you meant all that guff about what a thrilling, romantic adventure it would be."

"I truly did."

"And me being the only one you'd want to share it?"

"That too." A beat. "But mostly the bodyguard bit."

Chuckling, they crossed the road, and she didn't let on quite how eager she'd been to join his quest. Heading toward the Abbey, she glimpsed the iconic towers between the trees. They were too early for the exhibition to be open, so they paused by a War Memorial, pretending to read the inscriptions while he ran over their plan one more time.

"If you remember, there were several conflicting reports about the actual circumstances of theft, so our mission is to check whether the trophy is actually there from the start. But it makes sense to scope it out the day before."

"What makes you doubt the article which said it was stolen during the early hours of a Sunday morning while the exhibition was closed?"

"Because it was the only one saying that. All the others mentioned it being a literal daylight robbery, from under the noses of six security guards."

"But the woman who wrote that article works for the place – wouldn't you think she'd get it right?"

A shrug. "You would hope so, but one of the others went into great detail about stuff which I intend to check." He reminded her of the salient parts of the strategy.

The posters outside the Methodist Central Hall

advertised the Stanley Gibbons Stampex rare stamp exhibition, "Sport with Stamps," starting on the nineteenth of March. A smaller banner pasted over the top showed a picture of football's most famous trophy with a headline declaring, "See the fabulous Jules Rimet Trophy."

Having bought tickets, they joined the queue waiting to enter the side room where the cup was on public display.

"That's useful to know. If it *was* taken overnight, there would be no queue and the place would be swarming with cops." Georgie whispered in his ear.

"Good point, Watson." He barely moved his lips. "It would make our life a lot easier tomorrow."

When they were allowed in, the glass cabinet was flanked by two guards in uniform, exactly as the report described. Several signs warned against taking photos, but the idiot in front of them pulled out a camera and one of the guards cleared his throat and pointed at the notice.

"Oh sorry, I didn't spot it." As the guy made his excuses, Kev got close enough to read part of the notice: "Stanley Gibbons proudly presents the Jules Rimet Cup."

Georgie squeezed his arm. "It's so beautiful. Bigger than I expected. It must weigh a lot, the papers say it's solid gold."

The stern guard's expression changed as he bent close, his tone low. "Don't tell anyone, Miss, but that's not true."

With an exaggerated wink, she tapped the side of her nose. "Your secret's safe with me."

Chuckling, he stood back, swapping an indulgent smile with the other guard and Kev guided her out of the door.

"So far, so good. Excellent distraction technique, I

doubt they even noticed me with you there hamming it up."

"That *was* the plan."

"So it looks like the woman who works there didn't do her research properly." He sounded smug.

"I disagree. She was one of a couple who described it as silver-gilt. At least four of the papers mentioned a solid-gold cup, when it patently wasn't if you dig deeper."

"Ah well that'll be because they all used the same syndicated press release."

"You have an answer for everything, don't you?"

"Why do you think I make such a good detective?" He tilted the hat at a jaunty angle as they entered the main hall. It soon became obvious the reports of six security staff just for the trophy were wildly exaggerated. They only saw two other guards keeping an eye on the most valuable stamps.

Finding a secluded corner, Kev pulled out a copy of the articles, re-reading a highlighted summary which said the thief somehow evaded six security guards, removed a padlock, prised open the cabinet and stole the cup in broad daylight. He snorted. "Definitely a pile of exaggerated crap fed to the press to cover their arses."

"Pun intended?" She grinned, continuing while he tried to remember his actual words. "Of course there could be plain clothes guys mingling with the crowd."

"Hence the precautions." He scanned down. "Here it is. Police went on the hunt for a man in his late 30s with dark eyes who might also have a scar on his face."

Her eyes widened. "The guy with the camera. That description fits exactly. It could have been him."

"But why draw attention to himself? Makes no sense."

By the time they'd examined every display in the main room, Kev checked his Timex watch. "Still got a couple of passes, so I reckon I need a coffee. Can't stomach the idea of studying more stamps without a decent break."

~*~

Georgie could have put money on Kev saying a version of those words within an hour of them entering the place. They hadn't found out much about the Central Hall's catering facilities in the 1960s, but most tourist places had small cafés nearby if not in the venue itself.

Sitting nursing the dregs of a cup of builder's tea while Kev "did a recce for the building's rear doors," she reflected on the past twenty-four hours. Was it really only a day since Monday tea-time when they'd rolled home early in a state of intense excitement? At least, three of them were – Isaac had his dog-in-a-manger face on.

Kev had obviously done nothing but google stuff for the entire afternoon as he laid out his plans to go back in March and have a go at spotting the thief. He had it all worked out, appealing to her directly. "It makes more sense to use your dice and it'll give us more credibility booking into a B&B. And on the stakeouts."

"Hold on, stakeouts? With coffee and doughnuts?"

A grin. "If we can find them. But people are less likely to notice a couple canoodling than a strange man lurking."

"And they don't get much stranger. Especially when lurking." Jen's quip was a split-second before Ben's.

"That's me out, then. It was still illegal in the sixties."

"What was? Or shouldn't I ask?" Jen winked.

"Two men snogging in public. Or even holding hands."

Georgie sighed, torn between a desire to test out the mechanism for travelling to a different day and reluctance to do it again so soon. Along with a hint of exasperation at being taken for granted. But she sat back and listened to the ensuing debate about the plethora of potential pitfalls, slightly surprised by Kev's attention to detail.

Then Isaac stressed the importance of not meeting Ray or Pol, because they definitely didn't know them a few months later.

"Which is one of the reasons I'm suggesting we stay somewhere close to where the cup was found – it's miles away from Harlesden, so we're bound not to spot them." He really thought he'd got it covered.

So when she looked up from her musings to find Ray approaching the table, she had to call every ounce of self-control into play.

"Excuse me, Miss. Mind if we join you?" He gestured at the three empty seats.

Nodding with a weak smile, she fished in her bag for the headscarf which she tied around her head as he put his jacket on one of the chairs and went in search of Pol, who'd reached the front of the queue. *So much for Kev's certainty.* Scanning the room, she spotted him heading toward her and gestured for him to turn back while collecting her mac and handbag as her grandparents approached. She donned a pair of glasses to give a mousey housewife look.

"Sorry. We didn't mean to scare you off." Ray put the tray down.

She adopted an Irish accent. "Ah sure, you're grand. Me auld fellah's back from his travels, so the table's all yours."

139

"Thank you so much, you're very kind." Pol was staring a little too intently, so Georgie demurred with a wave.

"That was a close one." She steered Kev away.

"Was that who I think it was? You couldn't write it."

"*You* couldn't, that's for sure. Keep an eye out, because they think I'm Irish." She went to the ladies and changed her look yet again, removing the thin cardigan to show off the bright, sleeveless blouse. Red lipstick and a ponytail completed the transformation. She found Kev in one of the side rooms, dedicated to more obscure sports, after initially walking straight past him. He'd dumped the mac and hat, Brylcreemed his hair and added a pencil moustache.

She chuckled as they re-joined the long queue. "You look a proper spiv. They'll definitely remember you."

"Not with you on my arm." He leaned in. "You look crazy hot in that get-up."

A slap on his arm didn't dim the twinkle in his eye. "Oohhh, you are awful."

He pecked her cheek. "But you like me."

A woman behind them chuckled. "I love that Dick Emery, he's such a card." She winked at Kev. "But you're much better looking than he is."

He pretended to flinch. "Don't let my missus hear you say that, she'll have my guts for garters."

Georgie glared at the woman. "Sorry, love. He's already spoken for."

"You're a lucky lady, that's for sure." She nudged the woman with her and the two of them giggled.

"Not exactly a low profile." Georgie hissed.

He shrugged. "Can I help it if I'm God's gift?"

With a well-deserved eye-roll, she studied a painting on the wall as though it was worth that level of concentration.

After a second viewing, where he spent more time studying the cabinet than the cup, they went to a different room which hosted several years' worth of Commonwealth Games stamps. A distinct buzz of conversation outside heralded an influx of people, and Kev glanced up. "Sounds like a coach party. My cue for a final stroll."

Aware that she looked the antithesis of most people's idea of a philatelist, she leaned over the display case, surprised when an earnest chap in a white blazer approached, standing so close she caught a whiff of something unpleasant.

"Colourful, aren't they?" He pointed at the bright set featuring athletes from Papua New Guinea and she made a non-committal sound, moving to the other side of the case.

He didn't take the hint, following her round. "Many of the ones from the Melbourne Olympics are much more picturesque, wouldn't you agree?"

"If you say so."

"I do. I say, would you like to join the Great Britain Philatelic Society?" A tentative wave of his clipboard released a waft of BO which made her nose scrunch.

"No thank you." She pulled a hanky out of her handbag and pretended to sneeze. "Stamps aren't really my thing."

He gestured at the lack of people. "You must have some interest or you wouldn't be here."

"I'm here to support my husband." Another step.

"Oh. A girl as lovely as you *would* be married." His continual proximity suggested a personal-space bypass, and the hanky made no attempt to fend off the stink.

She glanced toward the door, thankful to spot Kev approaching with a frown.

"Is this chap pestering you, love?" He put an arm around her, drawing her past the worst of the stench.

She watched his inner tussle with the instinct to quip about personal hygiene, grateful when propriety emerged victorious and he muttered about moving on.

The guy could have given Isaac a run for his money in the social ineptitude stakes, as he grabbed Kev's arm. "You're a very lucky man to have married someone so lovely. The two of you are blessed with such good looks I'm sure your children will be beautiful."

Normally, he'd have shrugged it off as nonsense, but in an uncharacteristic display of peacocking, Kev puffed out his chest, smoothing back his hair. "Luck has nothing to do with it, mate. It takes effort to look this good."

"Effort well spent, if you ask me. And intellectually smart, too or you wouldn't be here." Mr Needs-A-Bath-Badly waved his clipboard, as he trotted out the spiel.

His eyes watering, Kev glanced at his watch with a grimace. "Five to twelve – we're late."

"Did you need to be somewhere? I'm sorry to have delayed you." The smirk said not.

Kev had already collected his gear and they hurried out. Georgie had the bright idea of checking the Sunday opening times, dismayed to find it closed all day.

"Drat. I'd forgotten about Sunday trading restrictions." Kev scowled, and she took his arm, steering him away as she pointed out they could join the crowds at the church service.

They walked back to the tube, but instead of going in, he pulled her past, heading for the River Thames. "What I wouldn't give for a camera right now. Imagine showing these photos to people. They'd freak."

"Because they wouldn't have heard of Photoshop?"

"True." A pout. "You don't *have* to suck the joy out, you know. It's not compulsory."

She kept her expression neutral, determined not to give him the satisfaction of a reaction.

"See? Doing it again." He punched her arm. "Lighten up, Pet. This is like a million times better than the best D&D campaign. We're doing it for real, with all the danger and excitement."

"Not what I signed up for. And there wouldn't be any if you stuck to the plan instead of–"

"Sorry, sorry, sorry. You're right, of course. But I can't help getting carried away by the thrill of knowing what'll happen next. It's like when you watch a movie for the second time – you kinda know what's coming up, but it doesn't make it any less exhilarating."

"If you say so." She scanned around. "You should calm down, you're attracting attention."

He followed the direction of her gaze, frowning at the gang of lads. "No, they're staring at you. Told you. Sizzling hot, you look." He leered.

"They're coming over. Do something." She didn't know what she intended, but it certainly wasn't what happened.

His face loomed close and then his lips were on hers, ever-so-lightly so they barely touched as his coffee-

143

flavoured breath teased her nostrils. Anticipating the effect on her balance, he gallantly supported her as she stumbled backwards, overbalancing so it must have looked like a full-on passionate snog.

Her arms shot up around his neck and she felt his lips curl into a cheeky-Kev grin as the lads heckled with whistles and cat-calls.

But it did the trick and they continued on their way, seeming to lose interest.

"Sorry, but please delay the slap until they've gone, otherwise they might fancy their chances with the old 'is he bothering you' routine."

"That's what you think they were going for?" Her brain couldn't fix on anything more pertinent to say as it reeled from the overload of sensory inputs. *Kev just kissed her!* Okay, some might say it wasn't a proper kiss, mostly because the prime motivation was all about putting off a dodgy-looking gang of lads, but even so …

Her body's response said it was anything but unwelcome – even that it was an experience she wanted to repeat. She'd seen this done in movies dozens of times – the unexpected snoggers would pause for a moment of steam-filled gazing, then they'd have at it.

But she just gawped at him as though he'd grown an extra head, and he stared back as though he wasn't sure if she would punch him. Almost as though he wanted to burst into tears because she'd stolen his ball on the playground. It was cute, endearing and the antithesis of the confident Kev she knew and … Whoa – where was *that* sentence heading?

"Georgie?" His voice seemed to come from a distant

source, and she realised her head was swimming and her legs had forgotten exactly how to support her body. As she tipped forward, he caught her, and she was once again wrapped in the divine scent of him.

Wait, what? Divine scent? This wasn't a regency romance novel and she was no love-sick heroine about to swoon. *Or was she?* Anything seemed possible after the past few weeks.

"Buck up, love. Reckon your blood sugar must be low. I did tell you to have a snack."

Trust him to leech the romance out and turn it into a science project. She scoffed. *But it's who he was.*

"Come on, Pet. Let's find somewhere to eat."

As they walked, she figured if Jen had been in that position, he'd have been all over her like a rash, having made no secret of his attraction to her. But he just saw Georgie as the very thing she projected – a surrogate boy.

She *could* blame a childhood spent rough-housing with her elder brothers and living without a mother for so long. But truth be told, if she'd had the slightest interest in "girly stuff," she could have hung out with the airhead bimbos at school who spent every waking minute fussing over their appearance or making lesser mortals feel like shit.

"Penny for your thoughts." He winked.

She grinned. *Granddad used to say that.* "I was just thinking back to some of the girls I went to school with. Wondering how they'd have reacted to this."

He snorted. "If they're anything like the ones at my school, they'd spend every nanosecond complaining about not being able to get a signal on their phones and taking those stupid pouty pictures. Wait – did we even have camera phones back in the mid-noughties, or am I just projecting stuff? I can't remember a time when that wasn't a thing." He squeezed her arm. "I bet you weren't like that – you'd have been one of the non-conformist rebels with piercings and tattoos."

"You mean not pretty enough for the popular crowd."

"Not at all. You have an inner serenity far more beautiful than Max Factor and Maybelline could ever deliver."

The speed of his reply smacked of sincerity, but her automatic protection mechanism had to tease. "Were they your favourite brands? I can see you as an emo boy."

"Don't knock it. When you're the runt of the litter it's either class clown or get stomped on."

"But the emos I knew didn't do humour. The opposite."

"I was like Kiss but without the makeup. And when I got pissed I danced like me da."

"You liked Robbie? Who'd have seen that coming?"

A shrug. "*Strong* was anthemic. When my sister got an MP3 player, I got her old Discman and I'd play *I've Been Expecting You* on repeat. He spoke my language, even though he came from a coupla hundred miles south of me."

She stopped at the door of the pie and mash shop, waiting for him to open it, like a good wife should. "I'm seeing a totally different side to you lately."

He paused in the action of opening the door and she was once again enveloped in his unique – and for some reason, enticing – aroma. "Right back atcha. And I'm not just talking about how gorgeous you look. There's something–"

"'Ere, mate, are you gonna block the door all day? Some of us want to get fed before they close."

The moment was lost as they hustled in, picking their way through a minefield of potential pitfalls as they sampled the traditional Victorian recipe of minced-beef pie surrounded by a sickly green liquor. Kev declined the jellied eels, but Georgie had a small portion – it had been one of her gran's favourites. The tables were very close together, making conversation tricky, so they stuck to mundane topics, like the up-and-coming World Cup match.

After lunch, Kev had a number of places he wanted to check out in his quest for the truth about the audacious theft. Georgie went along with it, a) because she had nothing better to do and b) because she'd become quite caught up in his boyish enthusiasm as an amateur sleuth. When they finally took the tube back to their digs, he led her on a circuit around the nearby streets, hoping for a glimpse of their target.

Georgie's patience, normally a large, elastic thing, stretched to its limits as they followed a third black-and-white dog. The owner jogged down the street, with no idea the habit wouldn't become fashionable for around two decades. It took a while before Kev could get close enough to verify the dog wasn't the one he was after.

But fate was on his side as, in the next street, they heard a man shouting, "Pickles." They spotted the soon-to-be-famous mutt snuffling at the scent left by the jogging man's dog. Georgie recognised the owner from the picture Kev had shown her, an ordinary guy who had no idea how his life would soon change beyond all recognition.

All the way, they'd been looking out for houses with laurel bushes in their front garden, and it came as no surprise when Pickles and his owner went through a gate next to the pungent shrub.

"That's it." Kev could barely contain his excitement. "In a week's time, some thief will come past here and chuck the cup under that bush." He shook his head. "But why?"

As they walked back to the B&B, Georgie had a few reservations about the next bit. It wasn't as though she hadn't done it before, but never with Kev.

She couldn't help but marvel at the way Kev handled things with the nosey landlady. His hair was still slicked back and she had to admit matinee idol was a good look on him. Little touches like a hand on her arm had the woman fluttering her eyelashes as he explained they might need to book for the following week, but it wasn't set in stone yet.

"Set in stone?" She frowned for a moment before giggling. "Oh, I see what you mean. It's a biblical reference, like The Ten Commandments. Very droll."

With an outrageous wink, he took Georgie's arm and led her up to the room.

Sitting on the narrow beds in the cosy twin room, she reflected on the tiny matter of sharing a bedroom. But hey, at least it wasn't a double bed like when she'd jaunted back to 1977 with Ben. In the event, he was every bit the gentleman. If he had any thoughts about following up from that kiss, she never knew – she didn't even catch him peeking. Lying in the dark, listening to his soft snoring, Georgie couldn't decide whether she was relieved, disappointed or insulted.

The next morning, Kev checked out after breakfast, and they returned to the hall, shuffling along in the queue of the faithful. They'd gone with their most nondescript outfits, adopting strong Geordie accents whenever they spoke. Once inside, a glance told them the side room was padlocked, and Georgie's trip to the loos included a peek through the doors to confirm the trophy's presence. So it definitely hadn't been stolen "in the early hours of Sunday morning," as the article claimed.

Somehow, Kev managed to endure the long service without too much fidgeting, but they slipped out before the end while the flock received their "bread and wine." They were not the only ones and, when they passed the side room, people had gathered, trying to peek in as one of the guards manfully held out his arms to stop them, asking them to, "Move away from the crime scene."

It was entirely possible the police might detain everyone still there, and they couldn't afford that kind of interaction with the authorities. Data collected, Kev took her arm.

"Come on, love. We'll miss our train."

Although there was no CCTV, they'd agreed there was no point in waiting around in case a guard had clocked the similarities in their disguises. He led her to a secluded spot in a nearby park to have a go at skipping forward a week.

They'd quizzed Isaac for any further clues about jaunting within a time period, but he was no further on than they, only ever having done it from the capsule. So it was all down to her focussing on the date and repeating it aloud three times. Easier said than done, especially with Kev's proximity and those dratted pheromones – or whatever they were – upsetting her equilibrium.

The first roll gave eight and nine, the second eight and seven. Georgie glanced at him, wondering if he would pick up on what was happening, but he seemed oblivious as he encouraged her to wriggle her shoulders and stretch out her arms before the next try.

After doing as he suggested, and clearing her mind before repeating the desired date three times, she couldn't help a tut of annoyance when the first dice landed on eight. But the second teetered on the edge between eight and return for a tantalising instant before settling on the return.

"Bloody hell, that was close." Kev blew out a gust of breath. "What would have happened if it landed on eighty-eight?"

"The results so far suggest we'd have gone to March 1988. Or possibly July 1988. Either would have been interesting. Especially if this was no longer a park."

"Shit. You're right. That never even entered my head."

"Do you think the rules about the limit on the number of attempts apply when you're not in the time capsule?"

A shrug. "No idea. But I wouldn't want to chance it. By my reckoning, you have one go left." His intent stare went on too long, tensing her shoulders and she wriggled it out.

"Sorry. I didn't mean to make you uncomfortable, I was just wondering …" He broke off, shaking his head.

"What?" She really hoped it wasn't what she was thinking.

"You'll laugh at me. Hell, I'm laughing at me just thinking how ridiculous it sounds."

"I won't, I promise."

Huffing a sigh, he spoke quickly as though that might somehow make it sound more credible. "You know how Isaac said your presence influenced me to throw all those sixes? I figured this is the same in reverse."

She scoffed. "Well, duh!!!"

"Yes, but there's more. When I – you know – kissed you …" His eyes avoided hers like they had laser targeting. "I – I just thought it may have affected your aura – or whatever it is – vibrations. Like, skewed the frequency or something." Another shrug. "Like interference when the ripples from a pebble hit the side of a tank."

"Whoa. You're verging into Isaac territory with the last two. Guaranteed to make my brain shut down. But as for the rest – I had the exact same thought."

"You did?" He preened. "Never had a kiss do that before – but you *did* start to pass out."

She slapped his arm. "Don't flatter yourself. As you said, it would have been low blood sugar."

"Anyway. I suggest we risk one more go. Maybe four is the charm instead of the normal three." A beat. "Because there's nothing normal about me."

The dice had other plans, landing on double return and whisking them back to the attic in 2022.

Ch 12 – Cromwell and Sealion

Sep 1940

Kev escaped relatively unscathed from the effects of a couple of jaunts close together, faring a heck of a lot better than the first return. Georgie, however, suffered a diminished version of Isaac's symptoms. Many of these could be explained by the onset of her period, which normally brought headaches and sleep disruption. She hadn't connected the runny nose, putting it down to high pollen count, but when Kev suggested she was starting to sound like Isaac, alarm bells rang.

They all agreed it wasn't wise to attempt further jaunts until they'd decoded more of the notebook, so they worked on the thankless task of trawling through their assigned pages trying each of the coding methods in turn.

When Isaac suggested a "fun" Bletchley session combining some of his previous ideas, they happily jumped at the chance of a night off. He started the session with one of Commander Dennison's pep talks.

"You may have heard some talk in the press about the extent to which the Germans have infiltrated the country."

"You mean like the recent broadcast announcing the church clock in Banstead, Surrey was running five minutes slow?" Birch relished the impact of his comment.

"Quite." The commander scoffed. "The bally nitwits actually went out and checked. I believe a council meeting was organised to investigate strangers in the town."

Birch winked. "Clever sods, those Jerries. They want us

believing every town is crawling with fifth columnists."

"So we have to be even smarter." Edward frowned.

"Which of course we are." Birch tapped the side of his nose. "Those chaps at Woburn are getting their own back–"

"The less said about that, the better." Dennison's glare at Birch turned into a self-satisfied sneer. "It means putting a hold on rehearsals for the foreseeable. Hitler's determined to invade, so we need all hands on deck."

June's eyes narrowed. "So was that just nonsense from the Times about him hoping the British government would accept his offer to end the war?"

"I read that article." Edward gestured with his pipe. "It suggested he considers invasion a last resort only if all other options failed."

"More propaganda." Clive snorted. "They made it sound as though the maniac considers us his friends or something. Utter tosh."

Dennison cleared his throat. "We've heard a whisper he's aiming for both air and naval superiority over the English Channel as a precondition for invasion, so there will doubtless be a massive hike in traffic."

"So it would be a real coup if we could get a copy of the latest codebook." Fleming had everyone's attention. "I reckon we should obtain a Nazi bomber and man it with a German-speaking crew dressed in Luftwaffe uniforms."

Edward clicked his fingers. "Just like that, eh?"

He ignored the interruption. "Then crash it into the English Channel, and wait for the Germans to send a rescue boat. The crew would attack them and bring their boat and Enigma machine back to England." A giggle. "It would be called Operation Ruthless."

"Operation Reckless, more like." Clive scoffed. "Just one small problem. If you drop a bomber in the English Channel, it would sink before they could get a boat out."

Fleming's face fell. "Oh dear." Then he brightened. "I'm sure there's a way of increasing the buoyancy."

Dennison's reasons for letting him burble on weren't clear, but the outrageous idea seemed to lift people's spirits as Birch clapped him on the back, suggesting it might make a good plot for that novel he'd been rambling on about.

The following day, news spread of a rash of hysterical behaviour in response to the codeword "Cromwell," which indicated a German invasion was imminent.

As they gathered for lunch, Clive read from an article in the Daily Mail. "Poorly trained local Home Guard commanders, on hearing the codeword, assumed the Germans were already on the beaches. They rang church bells, and troops hearing them took it as confirmation of an invasion in progress, and set extreme plans in motion. A vast chain-reaction spread across the country."

As predicted, the bundles of messages were unusually large and the crew meeting in the Drunken Arms that night were more subdued than normal.

Signing another form for Rhonda, Birch quipped about her selling his autographs for a profit. Then he addressed the crowd. "If I were to write a play about the antics of the Home Guard forces, people would leave the theatre shaking their heads at how far-fetched it all was."

Rhonda pouted at him. "Don't leave us in suspenders, darling. Do tell." She knew exactly the effect her words would have as every man in the room was now picturing a scantily-dressed version of her.

All except Birch, whose tastes obviously lay elsewhere. He cleared his throat. "These doddering old goats took it upon themselves to blow up bridges in East Anglia to prevent their capture."

"No. How droll." She tittered.

His next words shut her down, as he intended. "It was no joke. Three Guards officers in Lincolnshire drove over an unmarked minefield the zealots had laid." He mimed an explosion, making her jump, and she cringed at the dramatic finality of his tone. "All three dead."

Edward seemed oblivious to her distress. "Thank goodness those BBC chappies are on the case. They've been putting out broadcasts all day in an effort to spread the word that all is well."

She put her hand on his arm, gazing at him as though he were her saviour. "Thank goodness you're so well informed; otherwise I'd have been in a tizz all evening thinking we could be invaded any moment."

Clive spotted June's pursed lips as Rhonda positively simpered at the gallant chap's attempt to console her. He kept half an ear out as Hettie chatted to June about the excesses of the Home Guard, and overheard Rhonda quizzing Edward about Birch's oblique comment about Woburn Abbey. Thankfully, he couldn't enlighten her – or if he *did* know about the black propaganda coming out of the riding stables, he didn't let on.

Walking to the billet, Clive remarked how keen Rhonda seemed on Edward.

He scoffed. "I can see right through her. She flits from chap to chap, but I swear she's only after–"

"One thing?" Clive chuckled. "If the girls want to behave more like chaps, I say let 'em. I wouldn't pass."

With a blink, Edward cringed. "I don't think that's what she was after. At least, not from me." He ran his hand through his hair. "Oh dear. I'm not sure who to trust in this god-forsaken place. Everyone has an ulterior motive."

They'd reached the door to their digs, and Clive scanned around. "Why don't you come up to my room? I have a fifth of scotch I don't mind sharing." The hesitation screamed warning bells, and he chuckled. "Don't worry. It's not an offer such as Birch would make."

"Glad to hear it. You don't look the type, but …"

"'Nuff said." They crept in to avoid the other guests – their landlady was an early riser, so she'd be abed.

He gestured at the only chair as he poured a couple of fingers of the contraband.

Edward sipped his, closing his eyes with a murmur of appreciation. "That's not cheap stuff."

"American. Courtesy of my former air … associates." Clive swore under his breath at the slip, hoping he wouldn't pick up on it. *Fat chance.*

"You were going to say air crew. I *knew* you were a flyboy." He leaned forward. "I'd give anything to train as a pilot, but …" He gestured sadly. "This."

"What do you mean?"

"They'll never let us go. For starters, we know too much and if we were shot down – you know the rest."

"Don't I just." Clive swigged, letting the fiery liquid

blur some of the necessary training. "And, of course, you're far more valuable here."

"Tell that to my headmaster." A scowl. "Or those biddies who regularly send envelopes full of white feathers to my parents." He swigged, choking.

"That must be hard for them."

"Doubly so because I can't give them a clue what I'm actually doing. When mother read out that scathing letter, father looked grim until the bit where I was 'a disgrace to the school' and left the room without saying a word."

"Did he serve?"

"With distinction. Until he was invalided out after a double dose of pneumonia took half his lungs. He stayed on in a training capacity, but it wasn't the same."

Clive sighed. "They offered me that, too, and he's right. At least here I feel like I'm making a difference. But enough about past woes. Tell me your current ones."

Edward explained how he'd picked up transmissions from a German radio station. "It's called Gustav Siegfried Eins, but I'm pretty sure it's not real."

"What makes you so sure?"

"Because the little German I know suggests they are saying nasty stuff about Nazi officials which can only be taken as smears. Who in their right mind would do that?"

"There are pockets of resistance in Germany. Good people who have no truck with the atrocities–"

"I'm sure you're right. But there's no possibility of my home-made crystal set getting such a clear signal from that distance. I can barely get the Home Service."

"What's the range on it?"

"Around thirty miles with the full antenna, but I've only managed a short one here. Far too risky."

"But you told Rhonda you'd no clue about Woburn–"

"I didn't at the time. Lucky really, because I can't lie to save my life. But her quizzing had me adding two twos."

"So what about now?"

A shrug. "I still don't know for sure." He stared into the middle distance.

"I know that look. You've had an epiphany."

He shook his head. "Always supposing there is such a thing as a fake radio station nearby, would it be possible to get them to broadcast false figures about the RAF losses in the recent raids?"

"To what end?"

"Think about it. Hitler wants air superiority before he'll invade and if Goering thinks the RAF are nearly exhausted, he'll plan for another all-out blitz like in August."

Clive nodded. "He does seem the type to want an overwhelming triumph, but there would be no point hitting military targets if they're all but kaput."

"That's the beauty of it. He'd go for somewhere critical, like London – the beating heart of this nation."

When the news hit the following day, Clive was left with two options. Edward was either a brilliant military strategist, or a German spy. He prided himself as a good judge of character, and his instincts shouted the guy was a decent, honourable character who would rather die than become the latter. He listened in horror with the rest as the news told of the all-out attack on the London docks, describing how the burning buildings had lit the way for the waves of bombers through the night.

This led to an emergency meeting of the top bods as they aggregated the information for analysis, and Clive's special dispensation meant he was included.

Dennison gave a brief speech about the Germans' change of tactics. "Since Eagle day on the thirteenth of August, the simultaneous raids have concentrated on airfields, radar stations and other military targets." He pointed to the red flags denoting the recent attacks in the UK. They studied the huge map as he explained the blue flags gave troop activities in Europe and green showed the large number of river barges and transport ships gathering on the Channel coast.

"Their groupings will help our chaps to narrow down the proposed landing sites. There's no question they're preparing for an imminent invasion, we've never seen this level of co-operation between Army and Navy before."

"While the Luftwaffe knock out all our air defences."

"The question is when." Dennison's tone was grim as he ignored Clive's remark. "And it's up to us to work it out."

The explosion of messages swamped Hut 6 so badly the same grey faces and short tempers prevailed as four months earlier when the code had changed. This time it wasn't just June who took to not going home, merely snatching hours of kip whenever and wherever. Although it wasn't the height of summer, the huts were heaving with stale, stinking zombies.

On September eleventh, Churchill's radio address likened the following week to Drake finishing his bowls while the Spanish Armada approached. He spoke of the consequence to future of the world and its civilization, and bade every man and woman to "prepare themselves to do his duty whatever it may be, with special pride and care."

Fired up by these inspirational words, the flagging crew renewed their efforts, and were joined by Dillies Fillies, who were instructed to abandon their normal duties in an effort to get this vital piece of intel. A breakthrough led them to the fourteenth of the month, and this information gave squads up and down the country time to gather aircraft and crew in preparation for the biggest blitz yet.

In the event, the weather was impossible that day, but shortly after midnight, several small raids targeted residential London. The following morning, despite the low cloud cover, dozens of planes blotted the skies over Kent on their way to London.

The Hut 6 staff gathered around the radio to hear the latest as the BBC Home Service gave bulletins at 8am, 1pm, 6pm and 9pm. In the final one at midnight, a buoyant newsreader declared the Luftwaffe certainly hadn't expected anything like the resistance they met. He went onto describe how waves of bombers were unable to complete their raids on the capital, and those which made it through had little success in finding their targets in the thick clouds. A huge cheer went up, and Welchman recorded the latest figures of aircraft shot down on a blackboard which resembled an inverted darts match score as the numbers for both sides went up instead of down.

Two days later, all notion of secret-keeping was quashed as the news came through from the translation team that airlifting equipment on Dutch airfields was being dismantled. It could only mean one thing – Hitler was postponing Sea Lion. Shortly afterwards, this information was confirmed, although the new date was not certain.

The Duncombe Arms lived up to its nickname that night as the crush of people celebrating the small victory led to festivities extending long past the curfew. Even Dennison turned up, suggesting people get twelve hours' sleep before returning. He also announced rehearsals were back on.

From Hettie's encounters with mirrors, she had no illusions about her looks, so when Rhonda approached her to discuss costume and makeup, she was more than a tad intimidated, and listened to the advice and tips eagerly.

When it came to hair, she fluffed Hettie's dark curls, scowling. "Unfortunately, the panel *would* pick a blonde to play Margaret …" She paused, expecting a reaction.

It took everything for Hettie not to bristle with affront. "I'm sure Peggy got it on merit."

"Have you *seen* her acting?" She clutched Hettie's arm, tittering. "Of course. Peggy is short for Margaret – that must be it." A raucous laugh. "You should see your face. I'm only funning, I'm sure she'll be brilliant on the night."

Hettie frowned. "Why does her hair colour matter?"

"How well do you know the play?" A sharp look. "Act two, scene two. Borachio seduces Margaret on the balcony outside Hero's room and Claudio is supposed to believe it's really Hero being unfaithful."

"But we look nothing alike."

She produced two dark, curly wigs. "They only see her

161

from the back, and if you both wear these ..." With a shrug, she plonked one of them on Hettie's head.

Cringing at the musty smell, Hettie whipped it off. "That's dreadful. And itchy."

"I know, darling. We could try washing them, but they tend to get horribly matted."

Picking up the other one, Hettie cringed from the stench. "It smells like cat's pee."

"Probably is."

"They can't expect us to wear it. There must be others."

"Impossible with the lack of budget. And even if they could afford to, they couldn't get them because of this little war." Another shrug. "How we suffer for our art."

As Hettie contemplated the horror of it, Rhonda folded her arms. "Of course there's an alternative."

"What? I bleach my hair and she curls hers?"

"If you were to grow yours out, we could style it to match this wig. You have plenty of time, the performance has been pushed back till December."

"That sounds much better. I don't like the faff of long hair, but it'll be worth it not to wear that."

"Super." A speculative glance. "How are you getting on with the chap playing Claudio? Cliff, is it?"

"Clive. He's good. At acting, I mean."

"So he's no good at kissing, then?"

"No. I mean, I wouldn't know." Heat warmed her face.

"But I bet you'd *like* to know. He's a dish."

"Is he?" Hettie fanned her cheeks.

She nudged her arm. "You know he is. Even with the limp most of the girls would kill to have him chat to them

162

the way he does to you."

"Really? They'd kill?"

"Of course not, darling. You *know* how dramatic I am. But if you don't mind me saying, your scenes with him lack a little … passion."

Blood which had barely begun its journey south dashed back to fill her cheek capillaries, remaining there as the older girl described a number of what Gran called feminine wiles to ensnare his attention and enthral the audience.

For some reason, she scuttled off when June appeared, wearing a frown. "What did *she* want?"

"Only to give me some tips about style and such. Did you know she's acted in the West End?"

The frown deepened. "She's been boasting to anyone who will listen that she played to packed houses at the Palace Theatre, but I believe they were mostly revues."

"She's still had more experience than the rest of us."

"If you say so." A wink. "And done some acting too."

Hettie tutted. "Don't be mean. It doesn't become you."

"Sorry, but something about that woman sets my teeth on edge." She gestured to where Rhonda had Clive and Edward watching her every move as she demonstrated the dance they had to learn for the masked ball scene.

June all but spat. "When she's not flirting with every man in the vicinity, she's being nasty about the women."

"She said some nice things about you."

"To get you on her side. I swear she's up to no good."

"Maybe you should mention it to Clive."

Ch 13 – A Salutary Lesson

Aug 2022/March 1966

Georgie picked up on Kev's barely-suppressed impatience during the session, pushing for a comfort break. But she never expected him to enter her room without even a pause, let alone a request.

"Something on your mind, mate?"

"I want to do something, but I need your help."

"What could be so important you curtail a D&D session and invade my personal space?"

He held out an arm, showing how it didn't reach her. "You girls have taught us all about that – or has it gone up to two metres since COVID?"

"I'm not talking about the comfortable distance from my body." She gestured at the room. "*This* is my personal space, and people aren't allowed in except by invitation. I wouldn't dream of entering *your* room without knocking."

He blinked, glancing round as though registering his surroundings for the first time. "Sorry. I didn't think …"

"Obviously not. Do come in, Kev – have a seat."

He sat on the two-seater sofa she indicated, and she wheeled over her desk chair to face him.

"What's this all about?"

"I really want to go back to sixty-six and find out who stole that trophy. Now we know where Pickles lives, I thought you could take us directly to the evening before the mutt found it. Around ten o'clock should do it."

"I don't think so."

"No, you're right. We can't hang around there all night.

Maybe eight o'clock so we can book into a B&B."

"The answer's still no."

"Why? You were okay with doing it in the original plan, it's just we haven't figured intra-jaunt jaunts yet."

"What part of not overdoing it do you not understand? *You'd* be okay because it'd only be your third go, but–"

"Sorry. I completely forgot. With the D&D campaign being kinda time-travelly too, I got a tad complacent. Sometimes it's hard to separate the two in my mind."

She nodded. "I know what you mean. It's like 'fact stranger than fiction' gone mad."

"Perzackly." A grin as he stole Jen's cute mangling of precisely and exactly. "And when you add in the layers of role-playing, I'm quite expecting Kevin Bacon to turn up."

"You mean the EE mobile adverts?" She slid a glance.

"I meant the six degrees of Kevin Bacon. You know?"

A frown.

"The thing where every actor can be linked to him … you wretch. You're doing it again. So twisted."

Chuckling, she shook her head. "It only ever takes a frown to get you mansplaining. You're almost as bad as Isaac, but he automatically expects ignorance."

"You did *not* just call me as bad as Isaac."

"I did not." A grin. "I said *almost* as bad."

"Is that what you really think of me?" He glanced away, but not before she glimpsed the hurt in his eyes. Something told her a glib remark wouldn't do and she tried to give her answer the consideration it deserved.

But she hadn't reckoned on Kev's late-onset insecurities kicking in as his face wobbled and he jumped to his feet.

"There are worse things, Kev …" She reached out to touch his arm, but he shook it off with force.

"Not from where I'm standing. You're forever bitching about the way he treated you. Or is it treats you?"

She narrowed her eyes. "What's going on, Kev?"

He raked his hands over his face. "I have no idea what you're talking about. I'm the same old me I ever was – it's *you* that's changed." He stalked toward the door and stopped, flinging a closing retort. "And you've known me long enough to get that I never could be anything like as bad as him. I'll thank you to remember that in future."

He flounced out, leaving her slightly shell-shocked, jumping as Jen knocked the door and beckoning her in.

"What was that all about? I heard a rather different Kev to the carefree teaser we know and love." She sat on the sofa. "And he barrelled past without even seeing me. I just about scrunched back to avoid a nasty knock."

Georgie frowned. "Like he didn't even see you?"

"Perzackly. What's that about?"

"No idea, but he just barged in here without so much as a by-your-leave."

Jen grinned. "As our grans would say. You mean he pushed past you, too?"

"No, nothing like that, just followed me in as though it was the lounge or somewhere."

"Kinda distracted look on his face?"

"You got it. Never seen him so …"

"Single-minded?" Jen chuckled. "So you've never seen him playing a pc game, then."

"Right. Even in a campaign sometimes. But never in

166

real life."

Jen echoed the words simultaneously, and they bumped fists. "What did he want?"

"Only for me to take him back to sixty-six in search of that blasted trophy. He's obsessed with the damn thing."

"And risk getting health issues like Isaac? No way. He reckons the effects will be more powerful on us girls because we don't have the same body mass."

Georgie snorted. "The usual cop-out when it comes to anything from alcohol effects to calculating body-fat percentage. Don't get me started on that."

"Don't need to. I totally agree. *Gits*. But we've covered that rant a time or two. Back to Kev. Why involve you?"

"Because his dice will be primed for the eighties. According to Isaac."

"No they weren't. He threw all those sixes, remember?"

"But never sixty-six."

Jen hesitated and Georgie's head shot up. "What?"

She sighed. "That was before he travelled there. Reading between the lines of the few hints Isaac's let slip, it's all about connections. And what bigger connection than already having travelled there?"

"Desperately wanting to travel there again?" As she spoke, their gazes met and they both jumped up.

"Wait." Jen cautioned. "You think he'd go in the middle of a session?" A shrug. "We know how impulsive he is."

"Reckless is his middle name." She tutted. "How should we play it? I already told him I wouldn't take him there."

"We shouldn't let him know what we're thinking."

"What if he's figured out the connection thing? He

could go there and be back before the session resumes and we'd have no clue."

They exchanged worried glances, and Jen scoffed. "Except this is Kev – he'd be full of his adventure."

Georgie shook her head. "Don't be so sure. We had a similar conversation about Isaac not being able to hide his time travelling and look how *that* turned out. It's as though it changes people somehow."

"It certainly affected me with all those weird glitches." A shudder. "Thankfully, I haven't done it for a while."

"Suggesting the effects aren't long lasting." Clasping her hands, she sent a prayer heavenward, and they left to find Kev in the kitchen, sipping a beer as he asked Isaac how long the next scene might take.

Some things didn't change as Isaac smirked. "Surely you know better than to ask. I could talk about pieces of string, but I suspect you've heard it before."

"You could give a ball-park figure. One hour or five?"

He mimicked Kev's accent. "Why, you got a better offer? To quote your favourite line." A sniff. "As ever, it depends on how your characters react."

The scene resumed where it had left off, shortly after Claudio had denounced Hero as an approved wanton. They agreed to trim a lot of Friar Francis's long speeches, as the actor was struggling to remember them. Birch asked them to pick it up after the bridegroom's party had exited.

"Wait a moment." Rhonda spoke out. "Are you happy with that lack-lustre performance in such a pivotal scene?"

He frowned. "They took the direction and it was much

more physical this time. I thought it very credible."

"Because you're easily pleased. I saw no real passion between them – they didn't even look at each other."

"Because you told me not to." Hettie appealed to Birch.

"Well it didn't work." Rhonda glared at her. "Did you not listen to my advice? The problem here is the two of you are much too polite. There's only one way to solve this. Claudio, kiss Hero. As though you love and adore her."

They glanced at Birch and he waved a hand. "It's a known trick to improve the connection between the leads."

They were already standing as the scene required, so Clive seized Hettie's shoulders and tugged her towards him, kissing her as directed.

Although her first instinct was to cringe back, her senses overloaded with his enticing aroma and the gentle pressure of his lips on hers caused all manner of delicious memories to flood through. He *had* kissed her before. And it was wonderful. She sensed when he stopped doing it because he'd been told to and started doing it for real, but the sound of protests and loud heckling split them apart.

"*That's* what I'm talking about. Now run the scene."

This time, Hettie became the poor, wrongly-accused innocent, reacting to his harsh words with confused flinches which turned to uncomprehending tears. At the climax, when Claudio flung her off, Beatrice caught her so she did not fall, supporting her until her own father's harsh words, when she swooned to the floor.

"I'm done." Clive's abrupt exit ended the session.

~*~

Isaac wanted to discuss Shakespeare, but Georgie

dashed after Kev, leaving Jen to think up some excuse.

She raced up to the attic, opening the door to hear the distinctive sound of the time capsule's recording of *Doctor Who's* Tardis in flight. They hadn't determined the reach of the time-travel effect, and no way did she want to be accidentally transported back with no gear and especially with no dice for the return journey.

As she closed the door, Jen reached the bottom of the attic staircase. "Has he gone?"

"I reckon so. Giving it a moment till it stops vibrating."

"Good call. Hopefully, if he gets it right, he should be back by the time I reach the top." She started climbing.

Georgie checked the time on her phone. 19:37. Until now, she'd not paid much attention to the exact times they'd jaunted – either on departure or arrival. But something Isaac – or was it Ben? – had said suggested it was almost instantaneous, in which case, all should be well.

But they opened the door to an empty, silent room, and Jen went straight over to the keypad, where a scrolling message informed them of the lockout due to a recent travel event. "That's new."

"Is it? Or have we just never seen it before? Where's Isaac?"

"I'm not his keeper, despite what Kev–"

"I know. I just thought you may have seen if he stayed on the ground floor."

"I've no idea. Gone to his room, I suppose, why?" She gulped. "Shit. You think he'll spot the jaunt?"

"I'm betting there's a red light flashing on one of his monitors and he's watching us now. I was gonna suggest

170

not mentioning it, but I guess we have no choice."

"You never know. He might have a useful idea or two."

When they peeked into his room, Isaac had a map of London up on the screen, and when Georgie knocked, he minimised it. "I'm busy. What do you want?"

They piled in and, while Georgie sat on the edge of his desk, making him whinge, Jen snagged his mouse and expanded the map. "Planning a trip to Stamford Bridge?"

Georgie snorted. "Didn't think football was your thing."

He frowned. "Why football?"

"Because it's the football ground where Chelsea play."

His frown deepened. "That makes no sense. Why would he go there?"

"Kev? Probably because someone rang up the chairman claiming to have the trophy."

He shook his head. "What trophy?"

"The Jules Rimet. The World Cup?"

"I don't see the connection. I mean, I know you two saw the match and everything …"

"Do you actually listen to a word we say? I stayed with my gran and helped deliver my dad."

He winced.

"And Kev's talked about little else but finding out who stole the trophy ever since." Jen glared. "What makes you so sure he's gone there?"

"The tracker. Before the signal died, it ended up here."

"So not only do you listen and watch, you put trackers on us. Creepy much?" She shuddered.

"How else can I fix things when they go pear-shaped? As this jaunt obviously has, or he'd be back by now."

"What do you mean, pear-shaped?" Her eyes narrowed.

He gestured vaguely. "Dozens of things can go wrong–"

"What sort of things?" Georgie needed to pin him down.

"Oh you know. The sort of things which go wrong when you travel anywhere: you end up in the wrong place on the wrong day or at the wrong time." He giggled.

"It's no laughing matter." The girls swapped glances. "When you say place, you mean we could end up inside a wall or something?" Georgie could think of nothing worse.

He snorted. "Nothing like that. But you might end up appearing somewhere unexpected so people nearby get a shock. It's only happened to me once, and the woman was easily convinced she'd been day-dreaming."

"How can the time be wrong? I thought we had no control over that." Jen folded her arms.

"Not if it all happens organically as it's done so far when most of you have travelled. Grampy Eric was a firm believer that he could never be late for anything, because he was always exactly where he was supposed to be exactly when he was supposed to be there."

Georgie jerked, staring at Jen. "That's what the Ancient Oak told me in the Tangled Warren."

A shrug. "I've been hearing it a lot lately in various forms. Seems like a sound principle to me." She addressed Isaac. "So it's possible to influence travelling to a particular time and place?"

"Yes, but it's not straightforward by any means. Took me a while to get the hang of it."

"And yet Kev seems to have done it on his first go."

Isaac's pursed lips were his only response.

The girls shared another meaningful glance and Jen got back on topic. "Is that it? There's no chance he might have gotten splinched like Ron did when he apparated?"

Isaac rarely rolled his eyes, relying on other ways of communicating his exasperation, but this was a fully-fledged, sarcasm-laden, 180-degree roll. "I'm sure Georgie will have some essence of dittany if he does."

She scoffed. "We *do* know it's based on facts, and dittany does exist, but it's rare and expensive."

"And only found in Crete." Isaac couldn't resist.

She nodded. "But I have some of gran's ginger and calendula cream and a banana works wonders."

"Shame they don't travel well." He sniggered. "But I've never had any problems apart from the one time in limbo."

"Which is where Kev could be. Ben was gone for around ten minutes. I don't suppose you know–"

"Thirteen minutes according to the log." He gestured at the screen. "But it felt a lot longer."

"How long has Kev been gone?"

He checked the screen. "Eight minutes. Not a lot of point doing anything for another five."

"Except prepare to jaunt. I'll grab my bag."

"Wait. How do you know where to go?" Isaac frowned.

"I have a number of possibilities based on the extensive research he did. It'll all be there on his laptop."

"Exactly what were you going to do if he didn't return, Isaac? At what point would you have mentioned it?"

A knock of the door had Ben entering, asking casually if anyone had seen Kev. Georgie took her opportunity to escape. If anyone could rescue Kev, it had to be her.

When she reached Stamford Bridge, the gates were crawling with reporters who'd obviously got a whiff of the story. Everything she'd heard about the misogynistic attitudes was borne out by the wolf-whistles as she approached and cat-calls as she left. Without managing to get any useful information out of them about whether someone fitting Kev's description had been there.

One of them took pity on her. "You're asking the wrong people, love. For starters, you've just described half the men here, none of whom are prepared to share a jot of information without a price. One I don't believe a nice girl like you would be prepared to pay."

She saw no point staying, using a commotion at the gate to slip away. But she didn't go far, hiding round the corner as she closed her eyes and tuned in to the environment. When Kev told her about Ray knowing the instant Pol went into labour, it reminded of what Pol always referred to as her "fey" ability to sense when one of her boys was in trouble. Having had enough similar experiences other people would call weird – or possibly supernatural – Georgie knew she'd inherited something similar.

And Kev had obviously picked up on it when he cast her as Rosalina, the psychic, in his D&D campaign. Picturing him in her mind, she wasn't surprised that the first image was his face in the instant before he kissed her. Okay, he was playing Clive, kissing Hettie, but the connection was intense. It instantly swapped to his first kiss, here in London, only yesterday. On that note, she got the sense of. He *had* been here, but had moved on.

Opening her eyes, she peered around. It seemed no one was paying any attention to her, so she focussed on the next time and place, whispering it three times as she rolled the dice. According to all the reports, the trophy was found early on Sunday 27th of March, wrapped in newspaper at the bottom of the garden hedge belonging to David Corbett, owner of the famous Pickles. She recognised the house immediately, and gave it until quarter past eight before re-thinking. The plan was for them to stay in the B&B with a room overlooking the house which he'd already booked. But would he turn up without her?

While trying to decide whether to knock on the door of the B&B, she felt what she could only describe as a "pull."

Kev was in danger. Serious danger.

Slinking into the nearest garden, she crouched behind a privet hedge, thinking how her connection to Kev had been strong enough to override the time-capsule's protective protocols. Maybe she didn't need to know the exact time and place – it was certainly worth a go. Using the same technique to connect to him, she focussed on his energy, repeating "Take me to Kev" three times.

She'd watched enough thrillers to know her first priority was to seek cover, and there was certainly plenty of that in the run-down scrap-yard in a seedy area she didn't recognise as any part of London she knew. An angry voice had her ducking down behind the body of a battered blue car. Her eyes were drawn to a smear of red on the door, and above it the shattered safety glass had two small holes at head height. Not daring to look inside, she recognised it as a Ford Anglia identical to the one Ron Weasley drove into the Whomping Willow. What she wouldn't have given for some of *that* kind of magic right now. *Accio Kev* – wait, would a summoning charm work on a human?

Apparently it did as she heard his whisper.

"Georgie? How the hell did you find me?"

"It's a long story, but we have to get back now."

"Not until I get my dice back."

"Where are they?"

"In the office." He gestured at a dilapidated hut surrounded by several second-hand cars for sale.

"What's going on? Why are you here? Who's the angry guy? And what happened to your hand?"

He covered it with the other one. "It's nothing."

Suspecting he'd been in a fight, she desperately wanted to ask, but the crash of a phone being slammed down had him putting his finger to his lips and then it all went quiet.

She whispered. "How do you know he won't throw a double and jaunt somewhere?"

"Because he has no clue. And it's only one. Must have fallen out of my pocket when I hid under his desk."

"So he hasn't actually seen you?"

"No. I snuck out when he went back out again."

"Well that's it, then. We can pose as customers wanting to buy a second-hand car."

"That'll get you into the office, but under his desk?" A sly glance at her outfit. "It helps that you've gone for the 60s dolly-bird look."

She slapped his arm, then took out one of the dangly earrings. "It seems I've dropped one, sir." A flurry of eyelashes. "Would you mind if I looked under your desk?"

"Minx." The huge grin suggested he enjoyed this side of her, and she basked in the admiring glance.

Before they could act on what was rapidly becoming a moment, the door sprang open. A tall, sallow-faced man emerged, his expression taut as he jumped into a beaten-up Rover and tore off, burning rubber.

"Not a happy bunny." Georgie came down from her high as Kev thumped a fist into his palm.

"Holy hurricanes, Batman. He was in a hurry all right. Didn't even padlock the door."

With furtive glances all round, they nipped into the hut and Kev pounced on his dice, holding it up with glee. She grabbed his hand to leave, but he held back.

"We can figure on at least ten minutes before Betchley returns – you can help me search for clues where he might be hiding the cup."

"Edward Betchley? The prime suspect? But the reports say he only got convicted for demanding money with menaces, not theft."

"I know, but he was definitely in on it. I was hoping to find something on this man he called 'The Pole.' You know the routine – a scrap of paper in the bin, doodles on a pad."

"And exactly what were your plans if you found something incriminating which led to this Pole character? To pass it onto the police?"

A shrug.

"You can't shrug it off. Would you honestly have been able to keep it to yourself?"

He quashed the second shrug after his shoulders had

177

barely twitched. "Possibly."

She deadpanned. "Surely you've seen or read enough to know the potential problems with meddling in the past."

He glared. "You're quoting my words back at me?"

"Verbatim."

A police siren outside alerted them to their situation. Trespass was not dealt with too kindly back then and, if the coppers had already linked Betchley, they'd be in serious trouble. Gripping his arm firmly, Georgie chanted, "Double return" three times as she dropped the dice on the desk, snatching them up before they'd even stopped spinning.

~*~

"Thank goodness." Jen dashed over to scoop Georgie into a hug. "I know it's only been a few minutes, but it felt a lot longer."

"Where's *my* welcome home hug?" Kev pouted.

"Dream on, sunshine. You could have caused all manner of problems doing what you did."

"You have no idea what I did." *Thankfully.*

"No, but you're gonna have to tell us, mate, because something's changed." Ben rarely looked so grim, and three other pairs of eyes glared at him.

"Whoa. This feels like the Spanish Inquisition. Can a chap at least get a beer? I'm choking with thirst."

Isaac thrust a bottle of water into his hand and a phone in his face, the record button red. "What happened when you got to the Chelsea stadium?"

He swigged the water and stumbled over his encounter with security at Stamford Bridge, glossing over their suspicions and the fact he'd had to bolt. Instead, he told the truth – it was too early for the FA chairman to have gotten the note. Steeling himself to ignore the sceptical stares, he elaborated on his quick visit to library to read all the newspapers and diminished the hours he'd spent in dodgy pubs around Walworth and Camberwell trying to get a lead on the whereabouts of Betchley's business.

"Funny that. I must've called him Bletchley at least twice because of … well, you know."

"Yeah, and we also know you were putting yourself in deadly peril – those people you were schmoozing were all dangerous criminals. The Richardson Gang were at war with the Kray Twins, and you go around asking dumb-fool questions on their manor. Utter madness." Ben's sharp tone and period lingo couldn't cover his obvious concern.

Kev would never let on quite how much peril he'd been in – deadly was about right. But he'd escaped. And they certainly didn't need to know about the skills he'd learnt on his pilgrimage to the East to resolve his anger issues. These had definitely come in handy when he was up against it. He adopted a "lucky-me" expression. "Always better to be born lucky than rich, as me gran said."

Somehow, he persuaded them how innocuous the whole experience had been. He listened to their assertions that apprehending the thief would have changed history and have ramifications on future timelines, reacting humbly. But when they showed him the article written in 2018 by an investigative journalist, mentioning the actual thief by name, he struggled not to react. He couldn't be a hundred percent certain, but he would have bet at least a pony that the article wasn't there when he'd searched yesterday. So much for researching the crap out of it. But time had been tight. *Definitely something to note for future jaunts.*

Georgie listened as Isaac read from articles revealing that Sidney Cugullere was an opportunist thief who stole the trophy without using the slightest bit of force. He nicked it simply because he could and, despite the threats in the ransom letter, would never have melted it down.

Watching her changing expressions, Kev finally analysed why he'd sought out such dangerous experiences. It was all bound up in the warped need for punishment after the recent crap going on in his life. *But was he ready to face up to the real reason? And more to the point, did he have what it took to make it right?*

Ch 14 – Class Clown or Angry Thug?

Aug 2022/Nov 1940

Shrugging his arms into his shirt, Kev glanced over at the bed where the sultry creature stretched out, positively purring after another satisfying coupling.

Her full lips pouted. "Do you have to go, lover-boy?"

Months of training ensured his facial muscles gave no clue to his thoughts. He was proud of the neutrality – the quizzical eyebrow raised less than a millimetre despite the toxic mix of hatred, disgust and self-loathing seething in his gut. She knew damn well how much he hated that endearment, a relic of many years ago when he *had* been little more than a boy and she'd introduced him to the joy of sex. In the fabled words of Rod Stewart's *Maggie May*, she'd truly worn him out with her insatiable appetite. But the afternoon sun did so much more than show her age – it revealed her as the vicious bitch he'd spent years denying she was. He scouted for his jeans, discarded in haste.

As she employed her best seduction techniques, he congratulated himself on not being suckered back in – he'd come here with the intention of ending it no matter what. But he wouldn't pass on an opportunity to release the past few months' build-up of pressure. A guy's gotta do an' all that. And the stinging on his back should satisfy that bizarre self-flagellation urge – hopefully for the last time ever. A flashback to the scene where he'd had to inflict physical damage left a nasty taste in his mouth.

"Come on, sweetie. One more once – for old times' sake. You *know* you want to."

Actually, I don't. I've had it with your sick little games. Hard to believe, but it was true. The more he got to know Georgie, the more he realised a physical relationship could be way more than straddling the fine line between pain and pleasure. Although not as obviously sexy as the siren trying her best to tempt him, she'd got his engine running way hotter with her particular brand of earth-bound sensuality. Hopefully she never realised the effort it took not to ravish her when they shared a room. Her mere closeness had him fighting off impulses to rip off her clothes and …

"There's my boy. *He* knows what you want, even if you don't." Her treacly, patronising tone grated.

He pulled his jeans over the bulge. "Yep. And it isn't you." The zipper proved challenging.

She snapped her legs shut, sulking. "Whoever she is, she's welcome to you. I was thinking of trading you in for a younger model anyway."

"Good luck with that." He reached for his jacket.

"Oh don't worry, luck's the last thing I need. As you well know, I'm *that* good. I may even marry this one."

"More fool him."

"Fool is about right. Poor sap's besotted. And Mummy owns a castle in Scotland."

"I'd like to say it was nice knowing you, but no part of this" – he gestured at her and the bed – "could ever be nice. Have a good rest of your life, Maggie. Try to be kind."

"Kindness is the refuge of the weak and inconsequential and I can see now you're both. Just go. You sicken me."

The feeling really was mutual.

~*~

182

Georgie snapped her Kindle shut, having reached the end of yet another brilliant Adam Eccles book and left her rating. As ever, she was thrilled with the satisfying ending, and sad not to spend any more time with the captivating characters. She didn't fancy starting a new story, and it would be a while before the guys were back from rugger practice, so she let her mind wander. Like the hero in the book, she'd had her own inexplicable adventures. But she still felt exactly the same.

Jen glanced up from her Kindle. "'Sup?"

"Is it me or has Kev been acting strange lately?"

"Define strange." She winked. "With Kev, who knows what normal is?"

"I guess Ben knows him better than anyone. But I'm not ready to ask him until it's straighter in my mind."

"Whether you should sleep with him or not?"

"There's no question of that." Georgie deadpanned.

"Shame. I think you two are well suited."

She couldn't hold it any longer. "I mean there's no question because it's gonna happen any day."

"Yesss." Jen squealed. "What are you not telling me? Was it that kiss? I thought it looked pretty damn real."

"It wasn't the first time he kissed me. And it was definitely real. The most real kiss I've ever …" A shrug.

"You little …" Jen struggled for a suitable noun. "You've been holding out on me."

"Because the first time was by the Thames in 1966 and he only did it to protect me."

"Sound like some serious Disney. It didn't waken a sleeping beauty, or restore a beast to his princely self, but–"

"Technically that wasn't the kiss but the words."

"Whatever. Protect you how? From who?"

"A gang of lads who fancied their chances. I suppose, looking back, it was quite romantic as first kisses go."

"Hell yeah. Romantic full stop. I can't believe it took him so long. He's fancied you for ages."

"Kev has? But …"

"No buts. Ever since Warwick castle. Or even earlier." A glance. "Was that it? A kiss? Didn't you share a bed?"

"No, that was Ben. We had twin beds at Gran's and in the B&B."

"My how you get around. Sorry. Go on."

"He was – they were – perfect gents. Blanket down the bed and everything. Not so much as an accidental toe."

"Hmmm. I can believe that of Ben, but Kev? Mr I'm-Too-Sexy-For-My-Shirt?"

"Are you saying I'm just not pretty enough?"

"The exact opposite. He'll bed anything with a pulse. The fact he didn't try it on with you suggests he respects you too much."

"But he tried it on with you."

"That was different. He was just doing it because everyone expected it."

"Nothing you say will convince me–"

"Actions speak louder than words. That kiss wasn't just a peck on the cheek to shut Rhonda – I mean Isaac – up."

"No, it was Clive kissing Hettie."

Jen rolled her eyes. "Whatever. When you re-did that scene the chemistry was electric."

"When he threw me on the floor, you mean? I swear

that'll bruise."

"His eyes glittered with something akin to real hatred – as though you'd actually betrayed him. You know what they say about love and hate being sides of the same coin."

"That was just him taking on the director's notes."

"It was a lot more than that."

"If you say so."

"I wasn't going to mention it, because I thought it was just me, but I've noticed something different about him lately. Ever since we started this campaign."

"Go on."

"Don't laugh, but it's as though he's morphing into a romantic lead. Instead of the class clown, he's gotten kind strong and … heroic."

Georgie's eyes widened. "It's not just me, then. Honestly, you should have seen him back in 1966. Not at the football – he was just the loveable rogue we all know and … like. I mean, we're all used to."

"Very Freudian." Jen winked.

"When we went back to suss out the trophy theft, he was all kitted out like a film-noir private dick, but it was much more than the trench coat and fedora."

"I can imagine."

"Then he morphed into a proper spiv like off *Peaky Blinders*. But not menacing – he was utterly charming. Even had a couple of girls giggling and batting their eyelashes at him."

"I can totally see that."

"And when I caught up with him at the dodgy scrap yard, he kept massaging his knuckles as though they hurt."

"Like he'd had a scrap, you mean."

"Ha ha."

"Now you mention it, he's always had the look of someone my uncle called 'a bit tasty'. You know?"

"A bruiser. Yeah, I must confess it was *my* first impression, but the minute he spoke, I knew he was a regular guy, full of fun and mischief."

Ben poked his head round the door, chuckling. "This wouldn't be Kev you're talking about, by any chance? It couldn't possibly be Isaac and I couldn't see me ever being described as a bruiser." He leant against the door post.

"Where did you spring from? How long have you been listening?" Georgie blushed.

"Just got here. I dumped my sports bag on the floor and stuff fell out of the side pocket. As I scooped it back in, I heard Jen say about someone being tasty." He slid a glance.

"I meant handy with his fists." She frowned, waving her hands as though to erase it. "Not like a thug–"

A grin. "I get it. You can stop digging now."

"How come he's not with you?" Georgie peered out of the window to see if he was still by the car.

"He, er, had to see a man about a dog."

"You mean a woman about a booty call?"

"What? Why do you say that?"

"I spotted him getting in your car. No holdall and a smart shirt with his skinny jeans."

"Not that you were taking notes or anything."

"Haven't seen him all dolled up like that for a while. Ever since that Margie woman moved up to Scotland."

"Maggie. What do you know about her?"

186

"Only that he's got some kind of Mrs Robinson thing going on. When she says jump, he asks how high."

The violent slamming of the front door had the house shuddering in protest, and both girls jumped, wearing matching raised eyebrows as a stack of vicious invectives soured the air.

Ben tutted. "Oi, potty mouth. Ladies present."

"Tell 'em sorry."

"They heard."

Isaac dashed down the stairs. "Oh good, you're back. If you're up for it, I've got a short scene we could do before eating. I'm taking a leaf out of your book, Kevin, and paying for a waggy-mommy meal for all of us."

He might have not spoken for all the effect it had on Kev's filthy mood as he stalked into the games room and slammed the door behind him.

"Can I suggest you give him half an hour to cool off before putting the order in? You girls know the usual order, right?" Ben acknowledged their nods and followed him in.

"What did *I* do?" Isaac pouted. "I only suggested it because the scene fits perfectly with his current state of mind."

"Not sure it's wise to poke an angry bear. We've never seen him like this before."

"Pshhh. I believe he used to get like this all the time, he learnt some exotic techniques to get it under control. Can I leave it to you girls to order the food? But let me know when you're about to do it and we'll see if Kevin's over his little hissy fit." He trotted back to his room.

Georgie whispered. "Did you hear the bit about 'that

187

bitch playing him for the last time'?" A shudder.

"Wouldn't want to be Maggie May right now."

"Yeah. I hope it's not the fourth act again – I reckon in this mood he could do some real damage."

"Call me daft, but going back to what we were saying, do you think this angry-Kev could be anything to do with him going back to the 60s? Or even the 40s?"

"You mean like he's been affected by their nasty, misogynistic attitudes? That would be worrying."

"I was tossing between that and the idea of you going back to rescue him. Can't have been good for his ego."

Georgie shivered. "If you'd seen the way he acted, rescuing was the very last thing he needed. I'd love to know what actually happened, but my instinct is he's more than able to take care of himself."

"Another thing which has been bothering me. He must have spent a fair whack on that trip to the football, with all the bets and stuff. How did he pay for the extra jaunts?"

Her eyes widened. "The B&B's and tickets? No idea. And I'm certainly not bringing it up right now."

~>#<~

At the start of the next rehearsal, Birch cleared his throat ostentatiously. "Before we begin, I have a cast change announcement. "We're swapping the actresses playing Ursula and Margaret, so we'll start with the seduction scene."

Instead of showing anger at the obvious demotion, Peggy looked decidedly relieved, and Hettie whispered to June that she'd actually asked for the swap.

Rhonda revelled in the scene, playing to her strengths,

and every man in the room appreciated her sultry performance of a maid succumbing to the enthusiastic sexual advances of a ruffian.

Watching from the "audience" seats, June whispered in Hettie's ear. "It's quite obvious what she did to orchestrate *that* little manoeuvre. Apart from undermining Peggy directly, she's hooked her claws into Borachio to spoil the poor girl's chances."

The sturdy actor playing Borachio, instead of delivering lines with less sex-appeal than a limp dishrag, suddenly became worthy of the "luckiest man in the room" epithet under her skilful manipulation.

At the end, Birch addressed the two leading couples. "Now *that's* the level of chemistry I require from you lot. I suggest you pay attention to Rhonda's tuition, she clearly knows how to give the love scenes some oomph."

Only Edward seemed the slightest bit enamoured of the idea. Hettie saw her own distaste reflected in June's face, but she wouldn't have expected Clive's sour grimace. Particularly when the red-head clutched his arm and he adopted an alluring smile as he faced her.

She batted eyelashes. "I'm so looking forward to working with you, Claudio." A titter. "I mean Clive." She flicked a glance at Hettie. "And you, of course. I've seen some progress since our last chat, but I feel your romance could go so much further if you really worked on it." A lascivious leer. "If you know what I mean."

Clive glared at the hand on his arm until she removed it. "We're managing swell on our own, thank you very much."

Yet again, Hettie felt a frisson akin to trepidation at his

indomitable tone.

The narrator broke in, describing how rehearsals for the rest of September became sporadic due to another change of German tactics. The Luftwaffe gradually decreased daylight operations in favour of night attacks to evade attacks by the RAF. From October 1940, the Blitz became a night bombing campaign.

A surge in brown traffic led to a final breakthrough as Clive's knowledge of air-force protocols helped them to determine the exact use in controlling the X-Gerät radio beams as he explained to the top dogs.

"This peak of activity between noon and two pm coincides with the preparation of evening raids. The navigational beam angles for that night's target are communicated to the bomber units."

"How does it work?" Denniston frowned.

"The *Knickebein*, or crooked leg, is a system of huge antennae on French, Dutch and Norwegian coasts which transmit beams across the UK. These guide the German pilots to their targets at the intersection of two beams."

"Sneaky blighters. Do we have anything like this?"

"I never came across anything, but technology's advancing quickly in this area."

"Bally bastards. Tell me there's something we can do to intercept or jam these wretched things."

"We think they might be similar to the blind-landing receivers." Clive glanced at Edward who took over.

"If they're based on the Lorenz system, I believe it's possible to send a conflicting signal which will effectively bend the signal away from the target."

"Thank the Lord. Good work, both of you. I expect you'll be in touch with the London bods, eh, Foster?"

Edward nodded, but Denniston had moved on, clapping Clive's back. "Thompson. I'd like you to head up a section devoted to this brown traffic so we can send the target names straight to London and they can issue warnings to the affected cities."

Although stressful and tiring, the task was hugely worthwhile, with thousands of lives saved as people were given early warning to get to air-raid shelters long before the bombers arrived.

Because of the shift in message-peaks from midnight to midday, Clive barely saw his friends, so he was surprised on his return from a late lunch to see a shadow moving in his office. Creeping up to the window, he caught sight of a woman with dark, curly hair. Her back was to him as she sat on his chair, studying something on his desk, and his first thought was Hettie. Figuring he'd catch her in the act, he pulled back, but the crunching gravel had a different idea. All attempts at stealth forgotten, he hustled the few paces to the nearest door, hoping no one would spot his lack of limp.

As he'd figured, his office was empty, so he hurried down the rest of the hut, peering through each door, all filled with the usual fug of smoke and buzz of chatter as people got on with their business. A girl with dark curly hair would have stood out in all the rooms apart from the decoding room, however, only one of them wore it long enough to qualify, and hers was a much lighter brown.

He hurried to the other door and looked out, but it was

191

the shift change and the path outside was teeming with women of all hair colours and styles. As he returned to his office, he saw June arriving, shrugging off her coat.

"Do you know which shift Hettie's on today?"

"Same as me, we walked in together."

Thank God. It couldn't have been her. The intensity of his relief surprised him.

"We got here about ten minutes ago and I left her to go to personnel."

"You saw her at the mansion ten minutes ago?"

"Yes. What's this about? You look very stern."

He shook his head, trying to smile. "It's nothing really. Someone said a dark-haired girl was looking for me while I was at lunch and I thought it must be her."

She frowned. "Lunch? But it's after four. We were both at the house at lunch time."

He explained the different habits for brown traffic.

She held up a hand. "I'm not supposed to know any more than that. But I hear your team has saved several factories producing vital goods."

He nodded. "Not to mention many lives."

The door opened and Hettie dashed up to them, smiling broadly. "Two of my favourite people. I can't wait for the next rehearsal. Rhonda's had a great idea for that scene we struggled with." She fished out an envelope, handing it to Clive. "From Denniston. He said it was urgent."

Snatching it from her hands, he couldn't explain the sudden annoyance, but his eyes narrowed as he realised the envelope wasn't sealed properly. It was a top-bod meeting.

Isaac called a break as the following scene had the potential for "going on a bit." They were all invested in seeing where this unexpected turn of events might take them, so the food was demolished in a fraction of the normal time and they picked up where they left off.

Denniston had already started when Clive got to the meeting, and he caught the end of a statement that Hitler had taken it as a personal attack, and would be looking for maximum retribution to crush British morale. Glaring, he aimed the brief recap at Clive. "Last Friday. Britain's botched attempt to flatten Munich. Only success is showing our defiance. We're not beaten and *will* bite back."

He went on to explain how they'd decrypted a message showing plans of an unusual bombing operation with four unidentified targets. "The codename Moonlight Sonata suggests it will be at the next full moon on the fifteenth."

Edward nodded. "Hitler's obsessed with otherworldly phenomena, so it will appeal that this occurs on a full moon exactly one week after the attack on Munich."

"Quite. We have some degree of corroboration from a reliable source who mentioned a heavy raid, at maximum strength, was to be carried out between the fifteenth and twentieth of November and that the targets were to be big industrial cities in the Midlands."

Edward waved his pipe. "I read Goering had a theory that a major attack on a working class area would provoke an anti-war revolution."

Denniston scoffed. "The bods already detected beams aimed at the Rolls-Royce factory in Derby, back in June."

Clive gasped. "That's where they make the Merlin engines for Spitfires and Hurricanes."

A stern glare. "The anti-aircraft defences there have been strengthened and warnings given to other cities in the region, particularly Birmingham and Coventry."

"So we have six probable dates and four targets." Clive knew June would work out the permutations in an instant.

"I'm afraid it's much worse. A captured map indicates four potential targets in London and the South East."

As the meeting broke up, Denniston asked Clive to remain behind. "This is our chance to do some real good here. The instant anything comes in, we need to get it down to London ASAP." His raised hand stopped Clive's protest. "I know you're doing that already, but a message came in today with X-Gerät bearings which intersect over Birmingham, Coventry and Wolverhampton."

"But they're close enough that fighters can cover all three cities."

A hard glare. "The trouble is, Jerry invested a lot of time testing the system over the summer. The Powers That Be have been presented with too many beam intersections over the industrial Midlands where nothing happened."

"Makes sense, they'd have been checking the range."

"After the recent concentration in the South, the PM's far more inclined to believe the southern targets."

"A 'Cry Wolf' syndrome."

"You have it. But if there's any possibility of it being the Midlands, we need to alert them fast."

For several days he'd had a direct line to the airborne intercept squad and, shortly after 15:00 on Thursday 14th

November, they informed him they'd established the beams intersected over Coventry, and the beam jammers were switched on.

~*~

Normally a heavy sleeper, Hettie was a wreck after several sleepless nights – ever since she'd overheard a conversation suggesting her home town was one of the potential targets for some kind of retribution. From that moment on, she became obsessed with finding out as much as she could about Operation Moonlight Sonata.

One of the huge advantages of her job was that people saw her as a rather stupid girl, incapable of understanding anything technical. She did everything she could to propagate that notion, and her lack of the rounded vowels of the plummy debs ensured they regarded her as a small-town hick. And she was used to walking into rooms with all manner of top-secret stuff written on blackboards and flip-charts, appearing not to notice it.

No one knew about her talent for glancing at a page of writing and remembering every detail, but on occasions like this it came in handy. As she put an envelope on Clive's desk, she spotted something which stopped her heart. Minutes later she was hurrying out of the gate, tagging along with stragglers from the previous shift.

Ch 15 – Moonlight Sonata

November 1940

If anyone had questioned her reasons for leaving the site so soon after the start of her shift, Hettie would have been hard-pushed to give a coherent reply, but thankfully no one did. The chap on the gate was new and young enough to be flattered by the attentions of the gaggle of girls in high spirits at the end of their shift and no-doubt looking forward to the impending dance.

As she hurried, she thought through all the excuses she could have given for needing to disappear. But Miss M was a stickler for a "stiff upper lip," telling any girl who claimed to feel "under the weather," to "toughen up and do your duty." She had a bagful of mottos intended to inspire the girls not to give into what she called, "trivial maladies."

The light drizzle gave Hettie an excuse to be wearing her mac, but she left her handbag in her pigeon-hole, taking only the purse. She'd need more than the few coins it contained, and warmer clothes were a must, hence the detour to the digs. Her cheeks burnt as she recalled how she'd ignored June's surprised greeting, hurrying past as though not hearing her. It would have been nice to let someone she trusted know where she was going, but that would have made her friend an accessory to the misdeed, or whatever the term was. No way would she risk that – much better for her not to know anything.

A prickling sensation alerted her to the notion of someone following, and she stopped, checking her pockets, hearing a rustle behind her. Spinning around, she peered into the gloaming, uncertain if it was simply her nerves stretched taut by the many roles she was being forced to play. "Who's there?" Her voice sounded a lot stronger than she felt, emboldening her to take a step toward the noise.

A commotion of rustling, hissing and yowling hinted a cat-fight and, sure enough, a dark streak shot across the lane, startling her. "Oh puss. That's my heart you're attacking." She ran the last hundred yards.

Praying for no further incident, she met no one in the short time it took her to get to her room. There, she shoved on cargo pants, solid boots and woolly pully, all handed down from her brother. He also gave her his old kit bag, into which she stuffed a change of clothes and a couple of waxed paper-wrapped flapjacks. They would keep her going if something went wrong and she had to wait.

All the way to the station, her mind replayed the vivid dreams of the past few nights. She cringed at images of her mum, gran and younger sibling lying broken and bleeding in the rubble that used to be a house. Similar nightmares had played out ever since she found out about Coventry being a potential target. The first time, she'd witnessed the bomb whistling down from above, smashing through the roof of her family home, and crashing through the bedroom where her parents lay asleep. Each night featured a different detail, such as the windows shattering and bits of glass raining down causing rivulets of blood. It went from bad to worse as their bed collapsed into the dining room where she'd spent many happy meals. But the real horror was the second round of smaller, incendiary bombs which dropped through the holes, setting everything on fire.

Trying to rid herself of the horrific sounds, sights and smells, she paused outside the station, tying her hair back and hiding the ponytail under her coat. She pulled a dark cap over her head, tucking any remaining hair into it. Crude, but she hoped it would fool most people, adopting a swagger as she sauntered toward the ticket booth.

But she hadn't bargained on the eagle-eyes of an old timer who'd struck up a conversation, being originally from a neighbouring village.

"How can I help, lad? Oh, it's you, Hettie. Nearly didn't recognise you."

He shook his head sadly at her request for a return ticket home. "Sorry me-duck, you're out of luck. Last night's storms have brought a couple of trees down on the tracks near Rugby, so there'll be no direct trains for a day or two."

"Is there no other route?"

"You could go as far as Northampton and they may have another train to take you a little closer. Is it urgent?"

"Not at all. Thank you."

"You're welcome, ducky." A wink and then he was onto the next person in the queue.

Trying not to panic, she sat on a bench to consider her options. A chap wheeled up on his bicycle, and she wondered for a moment how long it would take if she borrowed one. She knew it was a little over fifty miles; probably around five hours. And very sore muscles.

She cursed herself for not being old enough to join the ATS and learning to drive. But the small matter of a suitable vehicle stymied her. The only person she knew with a car was Edward. Although sure she could persuade him to drive her, as with June, she didn't want to involve him. But what about the dispatch riders? She knew one who returned to Leicester shortly after five; maybe he would drop her off on the way. Checking her watch, she realised she'd have to run back to catch him and hurried out of the station. Of course, there would be a price to pay, but she knew he fancied her. If it meant doing something nice girls didn't do, so be it. She was past caring.

"It won't work, you know. Whatever you're thinking."

She stopped dead, seeing Clive leaning against the wall, smoking.

"I don't know what you're talking about."

"Let me guess. The trains aren't running to Coventry, so you considered stealing a bicycle or cadging a lift with the blond dispatch rider who's been trying to get into your knickers for months now. Are you really so desperate to get home you'd actually consider dropping them for him?"

The crude words and twisted sneer shamed deep into her core, and her hand shot up to her mouth. "How could you possibly know I want to get to Coventry?"

"Because that's what I'd do if my family were under attack." He dropped the stub and stamped on the burning tip. "Of all the things I said, that's the one you question?"

A scoff. "It merely confirms what I've thought for a while. You've been spying on all of us, haven't you?" She folded her arms. "Everything you say or do is about testing our integrity and loyalty. Well you picked the wrong girl."

"No I didn't. We know all about June, we're just waiting for her to make a mistake and give herself away."

Another scoff. "More tests? You want me to defend her

199

and give you the name of the real spy." As she spoke, she tried to assess her chance of escaping him if she ran. "Well I won't do it, I tell you. No matter what form of torture–"

"Torture? Oh, no, Miss Hettie. There are much more effective ways of finding the truth." He strode forward and kissed her soundly on the mouth, catching her wrists as she flailed against him. With his lips never reducing their constant pressure, he forced her to the wall, trapping her as he continued the compelling assault.

Against her better judgement – or will, as Beatrice would have it – she responded to his expertise. This triggered a change as he grabbed her hand, dragging her down the lane, away from the relative safety of the guards at the entrance to the BP estate.

"Where are you taking me?" She couldn't find any better way to phrase the over-used trope.

A villainous leer. "To have my wicked way with you, of course. If you were prepared to pay the delivery boy's price, then I ask no more or less for the same service."

"How can you possibly know I was thinking of doing that? You're not a mind-reader."

"No, but I *am* trained to observe and interpret body language and micro-expressions. I've seen him chatting you up on several occasions. And I happen to know he'll be returning to Leicester any minute … Oh – he'll have gone."

"Even if that were true, what makes you think I'll sleep with you?" Hettie struggled to free her wrist.

A wolfish grin. "I assure you, there will be no sleeping."

"You pig." She spat the word out.

"Oh come, now. Wasn't that your purpose all along? To

bed me so you can unearth my secrets? When you're not scouring my desk for titbits."

"I never –"

"Didn't you?" He pulled as she tried to dig her heels in, chuckling at her ineffectual efforts against his strength. "While it wasn't the most sophisticated of seductions, I must confess to a modicum of attraction and I do relish the idea of despoiling a virgin."

Her sudden lack of resistance caught him off guard and she fell against him, toppling them both to the floor.

He had no choice but to let go and, having anticipated the fall, she recovered quickly and ran toward the estate.

Cursing viciously, he got up and followed, making no pretence of a limp, shouting after her. "Wait, Hettie. I'm sorry, I didn't mean it."

She forged on, but his longer legs meant he caught up swiftly and he grabbed her arm, swinging her round to face him. "Please. I know I don't deserve it, but you must trust me. I'm on your side. I had to say those things to be sure … Look, there's no excuse."

She raised her free hand to slap him, then thought better of it. "*You* are a first class rotter."

"And so much worse. But please, let me drive you to Coventry. No strings, I promise."

"But you don't have a car."

"No, but I have a motorcycle. It'll be a tad draughty, but I can lend you some waterproofs to keep off the rain." He held out a hand. "It seems to have stopped, but they'll add an extra layer to keep you warm. Come on."

~*~

201

Clive held out his hand, hoping he'd done enough and she would take it. This had been a tricky one to judge and the natural anger bubbling below the surface had almost blown it completely. Thankfully, she had a generous, forgiving nature – or strong ulterior motives – and went with it as he got them suitably kitted out for the journey.

She'd ridden on the back of her brother's motorcycle, so she understood the basics of being a passenger, and his Triumph was a workhorse, so he had every confidence it would get them there safely. The difficulty of riding through pitch-black lanes was increased by the slotted cover which obscured most of the light from his headlight, deflecting it down to the ground. He was glad to reach the open road, giving him time to analyse the past few days, and in particular the last half hour.

What the hell did he think he was doing? The whole thing had gotten way out of control with him acting like the rake in a period drama. Right down to the cheesy dialogue. *Wicked way indeed.* What could possibly be going on in her head after such abysmal treatment? Did she honestly think he would torture her? A grimace tightened his lips as he pictured her expression, the trepidation saying yes.

She was right, there had been many tests, and she'd passed every one of them. He wasn't exactly joking about the effectiveness of physical intimacy in revealing certain truths about a person's character. Women who'd been tutored how to pleasure a man to the point where he lost control had no concept of the genuine pleasure to be gained from a simple hug or chaste kiss.

Hettie's reaction to his kisses said she'd not undergone

this level of training. Unless ... the idea she was so expert she easily gave the impression of naivety had no place in his head. A bump in the road had her squeezing around his waist and he couldn't help his body's response to her proximity. *Dammit, man. Pull yourself together.* The mission wasn't over until he'd delivered her to the destination and revealed her true purpose.

Clive knew which way he wanted it to play out, and flinched, recalling the grisly instructions in case of the dreaded scenario. Could he do it if necessary? Could he squeeze the life out of the woman he loved? This was not news – he'd known for a while how much she meant to him – long before their first kiss. He slowed to negotiate a dimly-lit junction, thankful the clouds had cleared enough to allow the virtually-full moon to light their way.

Part of his training involved learning about the lengths the other side would go to in creating the most resourceful, indomitable units. They weren't even considered people, merely assets, subjected to rigorous extremes and brainwashed into believing their actions would benefit the ordinary people in their country. Instead, the usually ruthless deeds merely increased the power and wealth of a handful of heartless masters. Having figured the perfect opportunity to confirm his suspicions, he pulled into a layby, switching everything off. He helped her off the pillion seat, then lifted the machine onto the main stand.

She removed her helmet, her angry gaze piercing. "Why have we stopped? And why here?"

"Sorry, but I need to loosen up. Can't do more than forty minutes without stretching. And I'm afraid this cold

203

had consequences. Do you need to pee?"

"Is there a toilet?" She glanced around.

"No. It's the woods or hold it till we get there. I only have one torch, so we'll have to take it in turns. I can go first to find a good spot if you prefer."

"I'd prefer a proper loo, but beggars can't be choosers. Now you've put the thought in my head, I have to go."

He couldn't fault the way she embraced the distasteful task without complaint, doubting any of the debs would have been so compliant. On her return he dribbled some water from a canteen so she could swill her hands and offered her a couple of squares of chocolate.

Her eyes widened. "Where did you get this?"

"An emergency store. Back in a jiffy." Walking to the wooded area required huge faith in human nature, despite his safeguard. Even if she wasn't a highly-trained operative, desperation might make her reckless, and she was game enough to risk driving it herself.

Peering through the bushes, he watched her pace up and down, figuring he should steel it out for as long as he could. As he took care of business, he strained to hear any attempt to start the engine, knowing she wouldn't get far. As he buttoned up, he saw her approach the front, and wondered whether she'd have the strength to lift the heavy machine off the stand. It would have been much more of a conclusive test if he'd left it on the side stand. *Bugger*. Cutting his losses, he returned, flicking the sneaky kill switch which would have scuppered any attempt to steal it.

Her eagle eyes spotted the move. "What's that for?"

"Just a safety feature to stop it from catching fire."

Her cheeky glare floored him. "Not a kill switch, then?"
He really *must* stop underestimating her.

~*~

June glanced at Edward's grim face as he pulled her into Clive's empty office. "What on earth can be wrong? You're scaring me."

"I don't mean to, but this is serious stuff." He got down on one knee. "June Cavendish. You don't know me that well, but trust me when I say no girl has ever felt like the other part of me – my infinitely better half. You complete me, June, in ways you couldn't possibly understand."

A grin. "I'm sure I'd work it out if you encrypted it."

With a groan, he reached up and kissed her lips before resuming his position. "I love you, June, and it would give me the greatest honour if you'd consent to be my wife."

"Why Edward, this is all so sudden." Her hand pressed her chest like a gothic heroine as she scanned around. "Are you sure this is not a scene from a play? It feels very …"

"Rushed? Staged? I'm sorry, but playing against you in Much Ado has made me realise how extremely well suited we are in every way." A wink. "I'd hate to waste all the time Benedick does in landing his Beatrice."

"Landing? I'm not an aircraft, you know."

"But I'd appreciate if you could put me out of my misery and furnish me with an answer."

"Did I not say? Of course I'll marry you, Edward. I've loved you even before we were forced together."

As he kissed her, Edward dreaded the next bit, but it had to be done. He broke away first, both panting at the passion they'd suppressed for so long.

She put a hand on his chest as he would have returned for more. "Are you sure this isn't just a ruse to get me to sleep with you? Lots of girls are succumbing, only to find themselves dumped as soon as he's had his wicked way."

"Do you really think so little of me? I'm hurt. Deeply." He raised the back of his hand to his forehead.

"Don't be such a drama queen."

A flinch. "Charming. But I promise, I'm nothing like Birch." He minced. "At least not so far."

"Ninny." She pecked his cheek. "I don't know about you, but I'm not one for a long engagement."

"Ah. About that." He rubbed the back of his neck. "I'm afraid I haven't told you the full story yet. For some while now I've had a hankering to do my whack for the war effort, and I think I'd make a good pilot."

"Has Clive put you up to this?"

"Not at all. But since talking to him, it's the one way I could join the fight without actually having to fight. I've asked Denniston a couple of times, but was told in no uncertain terms it would not be possible."

"Thank goodness for that." Another peck. "You're much more valuable here."

He scowled. "Hardly. And certainly not in the eyes of my headmaster." His voice dropped to a whisper. "Or my father." He explained how Clive was fixing it with Powers That Be, concerned as she blanched.

"So *that's* the reason for the proposal. You want me to wait for you." Her eyes widened. "Or is this just more pressure to get me in your bed?"

~*~

The next bit was a genuine error on his part, and Clive's only excuse was the distraction of his thoughts. Because Hettie normally did the journey by train, she was none the wiser, and neither of them noticed the moon was no longer on their right, but almost straight ahead so they were travelling north east.

A shadow overhead had him pulling over and cutting the engine. They watched in dismay as several ominous shapes were silhouetted against the still-low moon. They both counted at least a dozen, and Hettie whispered they looked like Blenheims. "But that makes no sense. Why would they be going north?"

"Because they're not the British bombers but Heinkel one-elevens. They do have a similar profile, but the leading wing edge is more curved, as though they have their arms down." He demonstrated. "The Blenheims have their arms straight out. And the tailplane is more of a sideways eight shape than the perfect oval of the German craft."

"I'll take your word for it. At least there aren't many."

"It's merely the start. The Kampfgruppe pathfinders light the target up for the heavy stuff to follow."

She stared after the squadron. "Just a minute. If Coventry's the target, why are they heading over there? I thought this road would take us all the way there."

He frowned. "Yep. I chose the 423 because it was pretty much due north all the way from Banbury."

"So why did you turn off at Southam? I figured you knew a better way."

"Because the signpost said … wait a sec." He swore violently. "Blasted idiots. In their haste to confuse Jerry, they went around removing road signs to major cities – or redirecting them."

"They being the Home Guard? But they were only acting under orders."

Guilt made him impervious to her perfectly reasonable assertion as he spread the map on the ground, scanning the skies before switching on the torch. Between them, they worked out where they were, and she suggested the most direct route, showing him how the southern bypass avoided the central area. She recited the remaining village names and road numbers, and he sensed she was committing these to memory.

Reaching the top of a hill, they saw bright lights in the distance which Clive knew would be the marker flares the pathfinders had dropped. He prayed the beam jammers had done their job and sent the planes off target. But he had little hope, having flown over Coventry at night and knew the sprawling conurbation would show up easily in the moonlight, despite the blackout conditions.

A second, much larger group of bombers had them stopping again, hearing a buzz akin to swarming bees as the tight formation headed toward the red/orange glow.

Hettie stared in silence at the scene which resembled nothing so much as a distant firework display as high explosives rained down on her beloved city.

He refused to budge until the squadron had passed overhead on their return journey, ignoring her folded arms and tapping foot.

"Come on, they're gone now." She tugged his arm.

"I really wish you'd think twice about driving into

danger. It makes no sense to continue. Think practically – what can you do to help now the attack has started? It would be different if we'd got here in time to warn them." The challenge was out.

She gestured, her tone fervent. "We're young and strong and you have transport. There'll be plenty we can do. Would *you* hesitate if your family were at risk?"

"No." He choked, unable to hold it back any longer. "Hettie. I have something to tell you."

"That you're a spy working undercover for the government? I'm afraid that's old news." A grin.

He shook his head. "I'm not surprised you figured it out. But I have to tell you–"

"That I've been top of your list for a while and you still haven't quite worked it out?" A sigh. "Shame on you, Flight Lieutenant. The clues have all been there if only you could get over yourself enough to believe them."

He put a finger to her lips. "If you'll just let me get a word in edgeways, I'm trying to tell you that I love you." Leaning in, he kissed her – honestly, passionately and because he wanted to. Releasing her, he was pleased with the sultry reaction before her eyes regained their mischief.

"And you'd still love me if I were a spy?"

"I'd still love you if you plunged a knife into my chest and these were my dying words."

"Now there's an idea." She brought up her arm and slammed it into his chest.

Ch 16 – Heroes and Villains

Nov1940/Aug 2022

Noticing the way Clive's eyes flared, Hettie couldn't help feeling a glow of satisfaction that his trust in her was so complete he couldn't see her as a cold-blooded killer. This was the only reason she could think of why his hands didn't instinctively rush to protect his chest from the knife in her hands. Unless he truly thought her a wet lettuce, incapable of violence. "Bang bang, you're dead." *Wrong instrument of death, but knives made no sound.*

His eyes flicked down to her fingers clasping the hilt, then raised to meet her gaze. Confusion morphed into the growing awareness of the pickle he was in. "But why?"

"Nothing personal. You are the master of tests so you should know."

"But how? You passed every one."

"That's the whole point about Mata Hari – everyone underestimated her because she was a mere woman." Keeping up the pressure was making her hand cramp. "You men will never know how easily you can be manipulated. The face doesn't even have to be that pretty and you're still thinking with what's in your trousers."

Amid his protests about how her beauty was so much more than mere prettiness, she saw realisation dawning on his face and prepared herself.

In a swift movement, he pulled her hand away, leaving not so much as a tear in the fabric nor pin-prick of blood. "What the hell, Hattie?" He grabbed her wrist.

She pressed a button, releasing an authentic-looking

blade. "Stage prop. The blade retracts." She demonstrated.

His eyes narrowed. "Who put you up to this?"

"I'm afraid that's classified. You may or may not be informed after my report goes in. Now are you going to drive me the last few miles or do I have to walk?"

"What, you mean this bit is real? You do actually have family in Coventry?"

"Yes. I've seen them in danger for several nights, so I'm going there no matter what you say."

Another wave of bombers passed over and, moments later, they shuddered as burning shrapnel pierced one of the barrage balloons, which exploded in a fiery spectacle.

"Eight o'clock. That looks serious. From what I can make out, they're focussing on the city centre. But there's not a lot of industry there, am I right?"

"It's mostly shops and lovely cobbled streets with medieval houses. And of course the churches – we live in an area where everything is named after the three spires."

"Quite a gothic cathedral if I remember rightly."

"Saint Michael's?" A shrug. "I guess you'd call it that. I've only been inside once – my family aren't particularly religious. I was only five, and it seemed impossibly tall and full of arches and triangles when you looked up."

The squadron flew back and they counted over thirty planes, undamaged despite the ten rounds a minute rattle from the anti-aircraft guns. Their journey around the beleaguered city managed to miss the next few onslaughts targeting the many factories in the north whose car manufacturing had been replaced by aircraft engines or munitions.

He had no chance of hearing her over the cacophony of sounds with air-raid sirens, the constant ack-ack and distant explosions drowning out the noise of his engine. Knowing this, they'd agreed a method for her to communicate instructions. A tug on a sleeve meant a turn was coming up, and just before the turn, she'd squeeze the appropriate arm.

This worked well until they reached the road housing the Alvis factory where all manner of uniformed men were dashing about trying to put out fires. An ARP warden held up his hand, circling a finger to indicate they should go back the way they came.

If Clive was surprised by her lack of argument, he didn't show it, turning the machine and following a side road for a few yards before stopping.

She shouted about the back way in, and he nodded to acknowledge, following her unspoken instructions as she guided him on a tortuous route around the back streets, fetching up at the gates of a park. An abandoned car was blocking the road, and she jumped off and peered through the ornate ironwork, pulling up the goggles to see better.

Light from the burning factory joined with the moonlight to show a hole in the roof of the large, double-fronted semi across from the entrance.

Ignoring his warning, she squeezed through a gap in the hedge and ran down the path as she'd done so many times as a girl. It was a much tighter fit now she'd grown, but a few scratches would not deter her. The other side was a different matter – the gate nearest her house had been blasted off its hinges by the force of explosion, and the other one hung crookedly.

She reached the path just as Clive pulled up. Oblivious to his shouts, she ran through her front door, which hung wide open, shouting for her parents. After checking the cupboard under the stairs – the most likely place – she tore up the stairs, opening every bedroom door to confirm they'd gone.

"Hettie." His cry echoed up the stairs, and she dashed out of the empty nursery as he prepared to run up.

"It's all right, they're not here."

"No, they'll be in the shelter like most sensible people."

"Unlikely. Mum gets jittery in crowds of strangers. But they may have gone to stay with her sister in Kenilworth." She sank down on wobbly legs.

"Whatever, at least they're safe. Which is more than I can say for us. The whole place could collapse any second." He scooped her up and carried her out, marvelling at the way the right-hand side of the semi stood intact while the left-hand side was open to the elements.

"It looks as though it went through the children's bedroom and landed in the dining room. An exact mirror image of what happened in my dream."

"Will your neighbours be in the shelter?"

"Of course. Mr Brockwell's an ARP warden, he'd make sure they were safe." She squirmed. "Put me down."

"I don't think so. You don't have the sense you were born with, running into a bombed building." A chuckle. "I suppose I should be thankful you kept your helmet on. It would have afforded some protection if plaster had fallen down from the ceiling."

She wrenched it off and flung it on the floor.

"I didn't realise you hated it so much."

"I don't. But they get in the way of doing this." She unbuckled the strap round his chin as she spoke, and removed his, letting it drop more gently as she pulled his face toward her and kissed him, holding nothing back.

Trying to support her entire weight and respond properly proved challenging, so he slowly lowered her legs without disrupting the rhythm of the kiss.

They both heard the weak cry for help from the wreckage, and she broke free, dashing out of reach to climb through the hole where the living room window used to be.

~*~

June and Edward sprang apart as one of the messengers barged in. "*There* you are. We've been looking for you everywhere."

They swapped guilty glances as the girl winked. "Don't worry, you're not in trouble, it's Hettie we're after. Have you seen her?"

"Not since we walked in together, but that was" – a glance at her watch – "hours ago. Isn't she on her rounds?"

"That's the thing. She took her first bundle, but no one's seen her since. Her handbag's still in her pigeon hole, but there's no sign of her mac."

"She'll be wearing it because of the rain."

"It hasn't rained for several hours."

"The cold then. It *is* November."

"I know you're her friend and you'll defend her to the end, but if you know where she is, please tell her to report to Miss M immediately or she'll be in even more trouble than she already is." A worried glance and she left.

June spotted the envelope on Clive's desk. "I'll take a guess she delivered this. Strange he should disappear too."

"Unless they're somewhere together." Edward pointed to the report underneath the envelope and she skip read.

"Coventry." June breathed the word. "Where her parents live. You don't suppose she'd be daft enough to go there do you?"

He scoffed. "Hettie? Daft is not a word I'd associate with her, she seems very mature for her age."

"Maybe daft's the wrong word. Concerned? Afraid? Her family's very important to her."

"If Clive's with her, we have nothing to worry about."

"What makes you so sure?"

"You *have* seen the pair of them together, haven't you? There's no way he'd let her go alone."

A frown. "That's no reason to assume … what are you not telling me?"

He raked his hand through his hair. "I suppose two heads are better than one. A while ago he gave me this, saying only to open it in case of an emergency."

"When you say a while …?"

"A few days ago. I nipped back to the house and his motorcycle has gone. Along with the spare helmet."

"Sounds like an emergency to me." She took the envelope from fingers only slightly reluctant to give it up. "It's not sealed." Retrieving the note, she read aloud. "If I don't return, please ensure C gets the enclosed message." A second envelope was also unsealed, the contents in code. "Have you decrypted this?"

"I didn't open it." He scanned down.

```
Xvzsfh mw s qoyh, rvwkahzj Gqjli
tyt zrtl packzj ZUH. Lilxir pcf
yfoozwnpnpc ti rrsqyxafm plhm as e
dscno cnifue - W dzuwigl Heaqkzxgf,
hie nv tec ti fbugpkf gltthg.
Yitwet: jkqlzwj og qttjmry lee kcz
wgek vzqf vzij lee. Zksp ugthtswl
xs arvrvvpkslk.
```

She frowned. "Looks like it may be a Vigenère, but what would be the codeword?"

"No idea. Look, we'd better get back before they send out search parties. I'll get you a copy and maybe you can work on it in between jobs."

"Wilco." She saluted, sneaking a peck on the cheek before scarpering.

~*~

Swiping the helmets from the ground, Clive plonked his on and closed the strap on the spare so he could sling it over his arm leaving both hands free. Following her into the large room, he was glad of the chance to determine the layout on the other side of the semi so he had an idea of the original geography. The cry sounded as though it had come from the back of the house, and he marvelled at how the room had remained intact.

When he tried the door through to the hall, it was blocked from opening, presumably by rubble. Another door at the back of the room led out into the garden, and this lay open, the footsteps in the dust showing Hettie's path. In what was left of the garden he listened, hearing her low voice making reassuring noises. He followed the sound, picking his way cautiously over broken crockery, smeared with the contents of bottles, jars and cartons. *The kitchen.* Barely recognisable under the top-floor furniture.

He saw her legs poking out from under a sturdy oak table, and bent down, calling her name softly. Touching her arm, he held out the helmet. "Here. Take this."

"Charlie, listen to me. I'm going to put a helmet on your head to protect it if any more things fall. It's a proper motorcycle helmet and you'll look really smart."

"What's the problem?"

"His leg is trapped by the dresser which is weighed down by the wardrobe, but if you try to move it the whole thing will collapse on him."

"Let me see."

She started to pull back but the lad screamed. "Don't go Hettie, I'm scared."

Somehow, she managed to scrunch aside so Clive could assess the situation. "Okay, Charlie. You've been incredibly brave, but I'm going to need you to hang in there a little longer. Do you know your five times table?"

A scoff. "Easy peasy. Five, ten, fifteen, twenty–"

"Excellent. But can you do it backwards from forty?"

Another scoff and he zoomed through it.

"You are a whizz. We'll have to give you something a little more challenging. How about counting back in threes, starting from a hundred?"

"Huh?"

"I'll start you off. Ninety-seven, ninety-four."

He picked it up from ninety-one, giving Clive a chance to hunt around the room for something which would bear the weight of the solid oak furniture. The table was the obvious choice but the weight of an iron bedstead made it impossible to move. His brain went into overdrive trying to think of alternative solutions, and he asked if she knew where the chap might store his tools.

"There's a shed in the garden. Are you thinking we could saw a hole in it?"

"No the vibrations would have the whole thing collapsing, But with some rope I might be able to haul the wardrobe off."

"You could wedge one of the dining room chairs underneath to stop it falling any further."

He glanced into the woodpile which was all that remained of the dining room.

"From our house, silly. Go next door."

It turned out to be fortuitous as, when he climbed out of the window, a loud voice hailed, asking what he was doing.

It was the same chap who'd moved them on. He turned out to be a friend of Mr Brockwell, and knew where he kept rope and useful tools. With two of them on the job, they managed to move the wardrobe, and Hettie had found the seat of a kitchen chair which protected the lad from further damage as the dresser slid several inches.

He screamed, and she got him singing nursery rhymes to distract him. They hauled the heavy dresser up enough for her to pull him clear, then gradually let it down again.

Hettie's gentle probing suggested a fracture, so Clive lifted the lad and she supported the injured leg as he carried him out, screaming with every step. It wasn't in pain, but for the stuffed rabbit he'd run all the way from the shelter to fetch. Glancing back, she spotted the grey fur and darted under the table to retrieve it. As she tugged to free it, an ominous creaking sound heralded the collapse of the final bit of ceiling, and a second iron bedstead plummeted down.

The narrator paused, aware they were all caught up in the drama. "Do you want me to throw for you?"

Hettie nodded, unable to speak.

"A three. Not enough, I'm afraid." He adopted a grave tone. "Clive turned around in time to see the life crushed out of his beloved Hettie." He snapped the book shut, expecting protests, but just getting a stunned silence.

Georgie leapt up and Isaac frowned. "Where are you off to? That was just for dramatic effect." He opened the folder. "We're not done yet."

"You might not be, but I'm dead." She shot out as the rest of them harangued Isaac about his choice of ending. She'd never had a character die before, and it was actually quite emotional.

~*~

"That was pretty despicable. You can't possibly expect us to carry on after that." Kev stood to leave.

Jen put her hand on his arm. "I'm not sure she's ready to talk yet. You might want to give her ten minutes."

He shook it off – anger, hurt and something dark robbing him of speech. Taking the stairs two at a time, he flew into his room, barely making it to the bathroom as his entire body heaved. But it was only dry retching, no doubt a reaction to the incredibly real storyline. He'd never been so invested in a character, and he had to face that the biggest part of it was the connection with Georgie.

Something weird had happened during the session and his visualisation of the journey through the darkness and the whole blitz scenes seemed very real. Especially the bits where he tormented and kissed Georgie – he meant where Clive kissed Hettie. And she killed him! Or pretended to. *Where the hell did that come from?*

Sitting on the side of the bath, he shook his head to clear it as he tried to remember, blushing at the corny scene outside the train station as they mined the tropes of all the "monster threatens maiden" scenes in old black and white films for the cheesiest lines.

Then Isaac had given them both authentic 1940s helmets to wear, complete with goggles, "just to get them into the mood" for the journey. From that point on, the whole thing had played out as though they were on a holodeck. He knew Isaac had a fascination with this idea from Star Trek, but … the thought froze as his brain replayed the last scene where the iron bedstead fell on top of Hettie, and his stomach lurched, the acid bile causing a second trip to God's big white telephone.

A knock on his door had him flushing the loo and rinsing his mouth, as Georgie appeared in the doorway.

"Kev? Are you okay? Were you just …?" She gestured at the bathroom. "Me too. What the heck?"

He strode over to close the bedroom door and pulled her into the bathroom, turning on the cold tap, his finger over his lips, whispering. "I'm pretty sure even *he* wouldn't bug the bathrooms, but you can't be too careful."

She peered at the walls and shivered. "I want to say this is overkill, but after that …"

"You mean the whole Bletchley thing? All of a sudden I know a hell of a lot more about espionage techniques – why would he encourage us down those lines if he was truly spying on us?"

"Do you reckon there was some kind of brainwashing thing in those helmets? I know they had holo-tech – I truly felt like I was in the middle of that dreadful night. It was so bloody real – the noise, the sights – I swear I even felt the heat from the fires."

He frowned. "Why brainwashing?"

A glare. "Really? You think it's normal for a girl like Hettie to stab the man she …" She glanced away.

"The man she loves?" A finger on her chin, brought her gaze back to meet his, searching for the connection he hoped existed outside of the game-play. Finally, he saw her unspoken consent and kissed her properly – not for an audience, or as a character, but alone, just the two of them. And it was wonderful. Of the earth-moving, worlds-colliding, time-melting variety.

At some point, and he couldn't have said when, one of them turned off the taps, and they moved into the bedroom – specifically, his bed. But he *did* know they hadn't been there long enough for either of them to get properly naked before a knock at the door had Isaac asking if he knew where Georgie was.

Her frantic head-shaking had him answering no.

Isaac tutted loudly. "I know it's late, but I need a debrief so I can decide how to play the next session. We'll reconvene in five, and if you see Georgie perhaps you can tell her. If you see her." Another tut.

Struggling to suppress their giggles, they shrugged on recently discarded clothes.

Kev cursed the man for his poor timing.

"I can't decide if that proves he has a camera – he made it obvious he knew I was in here."

"Well, let's give him something to watch." Kev dropped his jeans and boxers, mooning at all four corners of the room, while she cracked up.

"Prat. Think about it. He's never going to bug your bedroom, because of what goes on in here. But there might be a camera on the landing."

"And that, dear Hettie, is why you're a much better spy than Clive could ever hope to be. At some point, I hope to assert my manly authority and take you to task for all the times you cuckolded me."

"I'm counting on it." She wiggled her bum in his direction and he gave it the light tap it deserved.

"All right, minx. Come on. No point trying to hide this."

When they reached to games room, he cringed at the cheesy grins as Jen winked and Ben gave them a double thumbs-up. *His turn would come.*

Isaac rolled in a second later, with his most officious DM hat on. "From the reaction of at least two of you, I suspect you wish that particular campaign to cease. Is that the opinion of you all?" When people said nothing, he tutted. "If you won't speak, maybe a show of hands. All those who want to continue?" He raised his hand.

Jen, as ever became spokeswoman. "It's too soon, Isaac. What you just did was devastating. I don't know about the others, but I need to sleep on it before deciding."

"Me too." Ben agreed.

"I'm out. There's no chance of raising me with a spell–"

"More's the pity. Hettie turned out to be an excellent character. Full of spunk."

As the others swapped subversive glances, Georgie battled on. "–so I'd have to sit out any further sessions."

Kev sobered his features. "I don't see the point. I'm not keen on having to do any scene where Clive has to mourn Hettie's death – not my cup of tea at all."

Isaac scoffed. "I can't imagine it's a strength of yours."

June cut in. "I'm with Kev. I don't want to do scenes finding out about her death. And what more is there to do really? We know she was spying for the government–"

"*But do we though?* You haven't decoded the message from Clive yet. It might be something altogether different." A huge wink. "And what about Edward? Don't you want to find out if he got to train as a pilot? Or married June?"

Ben shrugged. "Not enough to draw it out for another session. It was pretty clear where their story was heading."

"*Was it though?* You don't know whether June might have done all manner of smart things with Alan Turing or Edward could have been shot down over France and ended up giving away the secrets of Bletchley Park. Oh–" he covered his mouth. "Now I've given it all away."

"So there's no point continuing. I vote to end it."

The other three raised their hands and he was outvoted. He stretched. "I don't know about the rest of you, but I'd quite like to get back to more conventional set-ups."

"Sez the man who just broke the format to pieces." Kev deadpanned.

"Sez the man who set the precedent in the first place." Ben scoffed.

"Hey, at least mine had a dungeon. And a dragon."

"Boys, please. It's not fair to put this kind of pressure on Georgie after she's spent ages creating her – what did you call it?" Jen glanced over.

"Fableworld. Kind of *Tenth Kingdom* meets *Once Upon a Time*."

As the other two groaned, Ben tutted. "Give it a chance, guys. It's got potential for some fun."

"How much longer are you gonna be working on yours?" Kev grinned. "I like the idea of a Marvel-based super-hero setting."

"I told you, it's Norse Gods."

"But it has Thor, Loki and Odin. Totally Marvel super-heroes. Or villain in Loki's case." Kev folded his arms.

Georgie stood. "Now you've walked all over my idea, I'd better get back to the drawing board. But you have given me food for thought."

"Food? I could do with some cheese and wine." Kev left the others patting full bellies and followed her out. "But we have a little unfinished business to take care of first."

She giggled as he smacked her bum, running up the stairs to her room which had a little more privacy.

It was going to be a long night.

Dear Reader,

If you would like to know what was in Clive's message to C, here's how to solve it. (text repeated below)

```
Xvzsfh mw s qoyh, rvwkahzj Gqjli tyt
zrtl packzj ZUH. Lilxir pcf yfoozwnpnpc
ti rrsqyxafm plhm as e dscno cnifue - W
dzuwigl  Heaqkzxgf,  hie  nv  tec  ti
fbugpkf  gltthg.  Yitwet:  jkqlzwj  og
qttjmry lee kcz wgek vzqf vzij lee.
Zksp ugthtswl xs arvrvvpkslk.
```

Copy and paste the above into the Vigenere tool at www.boxentriq.com/code-breaking/vigenere-cipher#tool,

For autosolve, I suggest Max Key Length of at least 19. Hint: the key is based on the informal name for GC&CS

Thank you so much for reading this story – I hope you enjoyed reading it at least half as much as I loved writing it.

If you did, I'd really appreciate if you could let others know what was good/bad about it by leaving a comment on Amazon: *https://geni.us/TTtimekicks*

Thank you
Jacky Gray

To find out more about my books, subscribe to my newsletter: *https://eepurl.com/b5ZScH*

For a teaser of the next story, read on:

Tarwen stood in the doorway of the aptly named "El Pollo Loco," letting her eyes adjust from the aggressively bright Mexican sun to the dim interior even as her nose twitched at the stench of stale beer, sweat and the rank cigarillos every man and his dog smoked. The first time they'd entered the place, many pairs of greedy eyes had turned and speculative lips had been licked as the men lusted after her long, lean body and the women thrust out chests in the hope of catching Aiden's roaming gaze.

This time, she barely rated a glance and the phrase about familiarity breeding contempt ran through her mind.

On her way to the bar she spotted him, sitting alone in what had become *their* corner, his brooding stare and lethargic demeanour hiding the keen senses which would be alerted to the slightest threat. Easily the most handsome man in the room, his startling blue eyes rose as though he'd sensed her presence and the subtle signal told her what she needed to know. *Apparently the barman spotted it too.*

The man's intense curiosity about them would normally have been disturbing, but he was merely exceptional at his job – a necessity in such a lawless place. By the time she reached the bar, two tankards of the citrus-tinged ale fizzed on the pitted wooden bar. Forcing the hint of a smile into her nod, she picked them up and strode over, sitting beside her partner so she, too, had her back to the room.

"Well? Did he stump up the extra five hundred?"

A shrug. "You know Santiago. Not exactly generous at the best of times."

"But he's taken a fancy to your … charms." He gestured at her tightly-laced leather bodice.

"This? I had no choice after you pissed him off so royally." She sipped the tart liquid.

"You think I should have let him ogle you without rebuke? What sort of a husband would that make me?" His chuckle met her glare.

"The sort who doesn't understand it's better to let men like him imagine they'd have a chance if only–"

"In what universe would a man like him ever have a chance with any woman, let alone one like you?"

Her sigh recognised the futility of arguing as he continued. "Maybe if you didn't flaunt yourself like a common–"

"You overstep yourself."

"Gah." He drank deeply. "They all fancy their chances. Like that eejit who hasn't taken his eyes off you."

"The one in the green cloak? I feel as though I've seen him somewhere before." Another sigh. As usual, he'd distracted her from the more pressing matter. "As to your earlier question, yes, he did pay up."

"I should think so, too. Five dragons in as many days are worth every cent of the bonus."

"It's purely to keep us sweet for the next mission."

At that instant, the door burst open, admitting a short, thickset man who barrelled towards them. A heartbeat later, green-cloak was on an intercept path with the newcomer, his intention obvious.

Before she had time to draw her weapon, Aiden had his knife at the throat of the stranger, who sprawled on the floor, the dark cloak spread beneath him.

Also by Jacky Gray

Time Doctors – Time-Travel meets Dungeons & Dragons
Time and Time Again
Just in Time
Time Kicks Back – Coming 2023

Calamity chicks 70s Sweethearts
Tina's Torment – Ugly Duckling
Chloe's Chaos – Goldilocks
Linda's Lament – Reluctant Rockstar

Bryant Rockwell – YA Contemporary Romance
New Kid in Town
The Show Must Go On
Leader of the Pack
Edge of the Blade
Music was my First Love
Stand by Me
Indivisible – BR Boxset #1-3
Invincible – BR Boxset #4-6

If you like historical-*ish* stories, Archer's magical world is now a 13-book saga featuring 3 different series:

Nature's Tribe – *Medieval Fantasy Saga*
3 Handfastings and a Burial – Wedding-themed shorts
12 Days of Yule – A Christmas-themed romance
8 Sabbats of the Year – A seasonal-themed romance
13 Esbats of the Moon – Dystopian origin story
Nature's Tribe Boxset – Books 1-4+Bonus short story

Hengist – *Medieval-alternate-world Fantasy*
Archer – A sensitive warrior
Rory – A lonely misfit
Reagan – An intrepid geek
Slater – A courageous time-traveller
Geraint – A reluctant heir
Archer's Quest – Books 1-2+Bad Boys
Uniting the Tribes – Books 3-5+Good Guys

Colour of Light – *the final series in the Hengist saga.*
Context – Short stories of rebellion & redemption
Chrysalis – Medieval magic meets modern-day mystery
Captive – Modern-day mystery meets medieval magic
Catalyst – Medieval magic meets modern military thriller
Colour of Light Boxset – Books 1-4+Bonus short story

Acknowledgments

Huge thanks to all the people who have supported me with constructive comments and suggestions. Special thanks to Paul for his technical expertise and Katy, Andrea and Tracy, for seeing off the (many) gremlins – really couldn't do this without you wonderful people brightening my days.

Big shout out to the fabulous GetCovers designers for the awesome cover. And thanks to Keith and all those from his awesome Broadhall Club who have helped out: Adrian, Vickie, Georgie, Oso, Adam, Stuart, Frank, Ray, Andy and Duncan. A big apology to my family who have suffered the sight of me chained to my lap-top for many more hours than they ought to have endured. But the biggest thanks go to all my readers – especially those who put a review on Amazon. *Thank You.*

About the Author

Jacky Gray's first career was telecoms and after 23 years writing software, she spent 17 years teaching kids, occasionally introducing them to the joy of maths. Teaching is now ancient history – a bit like the books she writes. Well, most of them.

Jacky lives in the English Midlands with her husband and the youngest of three grown-up children. She enjoys all live entertainment, watches a lot of movies and some great TV shows like GoT, Merlin, Robin Hood, and anything remotely Marvel. She listens to a lot of Journey and Queen and reads (apologies to the adverb police) voraciously.

About the Story

This was pure joy from start to finish. What's not to like about spending time among spies and heroes? I thoroughly recommend a visit to Bletchley Park, and there are several movies/TV series devoted to this stuff. Any resemblance to people who think they know me is pure coincidence – I borrowed some of your story, not your life.

And to give you a further hint

GC&CS was known as: Golf, Cheese & Chess Society

If it still fails, checkout this link to the decode: https://hengistpeoplehorse.blogspot.com/p/time-kicks-back-secret-messages.html#Ch16msg

Printed in Great Britain
by Amazon

41801457R00138